ROYAL CHARMER

KYLIE GILMORE

First Edition: June 2019

Cover design by Michele Catalano Creative

Published by: Extra Fancy Books

ISBN-10: 1-942238-90-8

ISBN-13: 978-1-942238-90-4

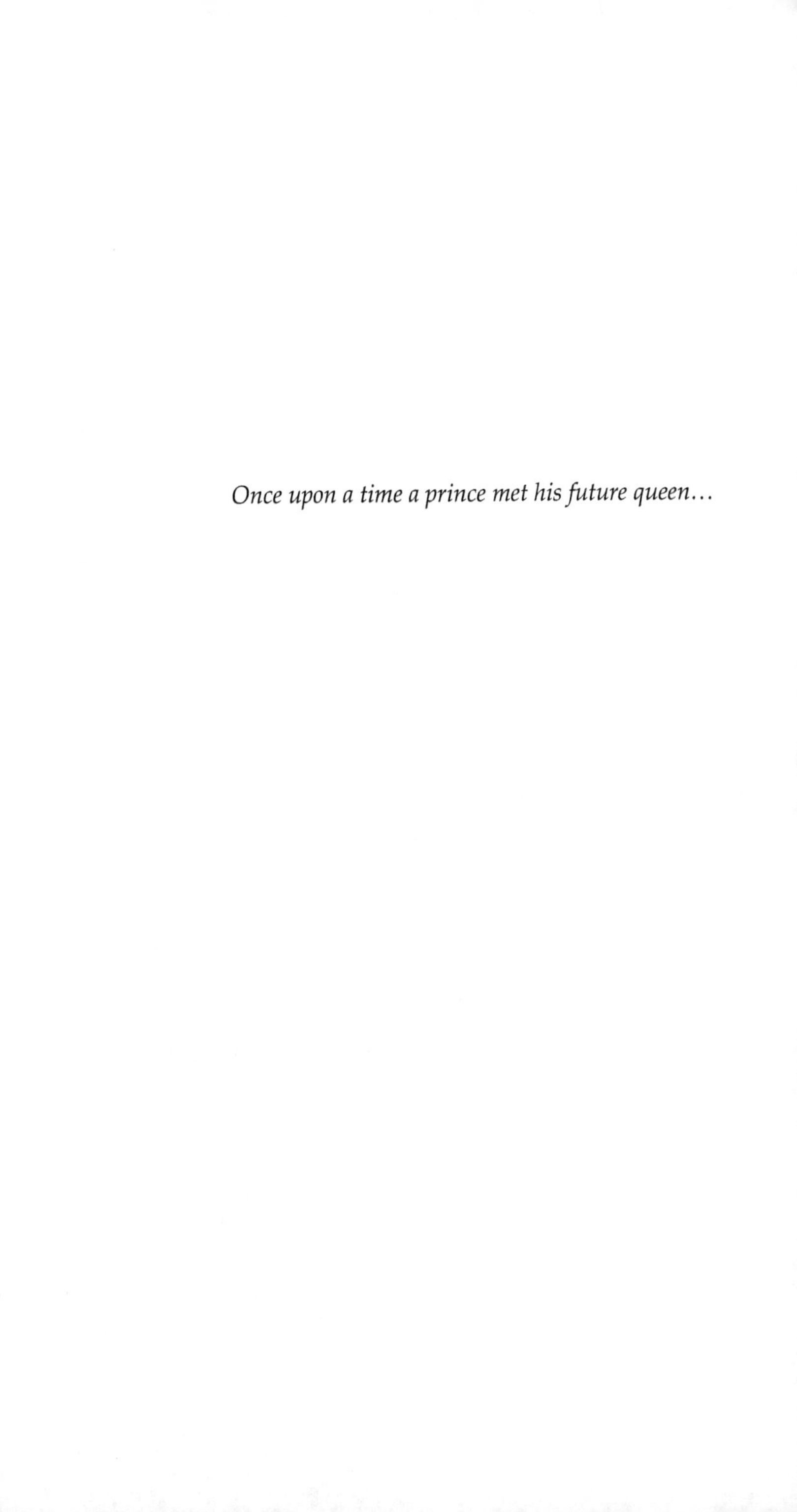

Once upon a time a prince met his future queen…

1

____

Alice

Only a badass would go on their honeymoon sans groom.

This is proof that I, Alice Segal, am a badass. You heard it here first, folks. You knock me down and I just get back up again stronger than ever. I can hardly believe I'm really here in the royal honeymoon suite of an honest-to-God palace on Villroy Island. I throw back the white duvet cover and sit up in my amazing four-poster hand-carved mahogany bed. A sheer white gauzy canopy overhead adds to the dreamy romantic feeling. And I know romance. I'm a historical romance author.

I snag my cat's-eye glasses with silver hearts from the nightstand and slip them on. This two-hour nap can't touch my sleep deprivation, but at least my brain is functioning again. I only dozed for a few hours during the long flight from Portland, Oregon. When I arrived here on Villroy Island, just off the coast of southwestern France, I figured a short nap would get me on the local time right away. I've got a full day of work ahead. Here's the thing—I need this getaway for inspiration. My next book is due, like, yesterday to my publisher, and I haven't written one word. First, I was too caught up in wedding preparations, and then, after

Mason called the wedding off last week, I couldn't even get off the sofa. My devout belief in romance is shattered, as is my heart, my soul, and my faith in humanity. I don't want to talk about it.

Suffice it to say, I *love* love, always have, and Mason killed that for me. Probably the worst thing you could do to a romance author on a deadline (or any woman with a beating heart). I force a deep breath and blink back threatening tears. I'm done with that now. Really. I've grieved and I've moved on.

Here are the facts:

1. Mason and I were together for a year, six months of which we were engaged.

2. He cheated on me with Riley for the last three months, unbeknownst to me, *while we were engaged.*

3. Riley has been my best friend since middle school.

She was the extrovert to my introvert, a deeply trusted confidante, and the one person I could always turn to. Except how can you turn to your best friend when you're devastated over something she did?

The good news is—yes, there is good news, which is why I'm not currently curled up in a ball crying my eyes out—I just woke up with a fantastic idea in my head. My editor will be so pleased. Even if I turn in a rougher draft than usual, as long as I turn something in by the deadline, two weeks from now, I'm good. I never planned to write on my honeymoon, yet here I am, trying really hard not to freak out. It's write-the-damn-book-or-get-fired time. This is the much anticipated third book in a trilogy set in Regency England. I grab my phone and call my editor, Quinn, to share the good news. We're close, and I just know her excitement will feed mine and bring back my much-missed writing mojo. Voicemail.

Okay, no problem. I will use this time productively. I pull out a small notepad and scribble down my idea before it can scamper away; then I tour the guest suite, taking notes. I was too tired before to really take it in. It's not often you get a chance to stay at a centuries-old palace. Since the honeymoon was already paid in full, I went for it, figuring the change of scenery would be just what I needed, and so far that's true. I'll use some of the details of the suite for my hero's residence. It really is lovely. The master bedroom is filled with antique mahogany furniture with elaborate carvings. Golden sconces on the walls resemble candles, and there are two shimmery light gold columns on either side of the bed, with adorable cherubs perched on top. I sniff the air. It smells like lavender, a soothing scent. Perfect.

A round table holds a crystal vase of roses, an ice bucket, and a single champagne flute. Only one thick white robe hangs in the wardrobe. I called ahead to mention I was traveling solo, and it's nice not to have couple reminders. Otherwise, I might get stabby. Ha-ha. No worries. I'm mostly stable.

I wander into the living room of the suite, my eye catching on a fantastical sea painting on the ceiling with mermaids and nymphs. Riley and I used to puzzle over mermaids and how they had sex. This was during the height of our middle school obsession with fantasy creatures. I stare straight ahead, collecting myself for a moment, but my chest still feels tight like Mason and Riley are sitting on my lungs, gazing lovingly into each other's eyes. I need fresh air.

I grab my phone and stuff it into the pocket of my pretty pink with white flowers travel dress. I love this dress mostly because it's super roomy, long, and it has pockets. I'm what you call a curvy girl, though I don't know why people must reference me in terms of my body in the first place. Unfortunately, I have seen that description more than once in articles written about me (also full-figured and plus-size woman). Who cares if I shop in the plus-size section? Plus what? Comfortable reasonably sized material? I'd much prefer to be called an interesting woman or a witty smart woman, which I am, than a curvy or plus-size one. I blame the patriarchy. Also Hollywood, fashion, and just about every women's magazine. Hmph. I slip my feet into my black chunky-heeled sandals and head to the mirror, where I smooth my nap-rumpled dirty-blond hair down. I lean closer, lowering my glasses down my nose for a better look at—damn, there *are* bags under my eyes. I'm twenty-three, much too young for bags. I shove my glasses back in place. I just need one good night's sleep and that will clear right up.

I whirl and head straight out the door of my suite.

A maid appears out of nowhere in the white button-down shirt and black pants all the servants wear around here. I'd been hoping for something a little more traditional in the way of uniforms. I pictured the maids in black dresses with white frilly aprons, along with footmen in formal coats with tails, and a butler in a tux. At least the butler was wearing a black suit.

She smiles. "Hello, ma'am, I'm Christina. May I help you with something?"

"Hello." I point down the hallway. "I'm just going out for some fresh air."

"Ah. You might enjoy the palace courtyard. It leads to the formal gardens."

"Wonderful. If you could just point me in the right direction."

She begins an elaborate description of twists and turns and landmarks along the way that quickly turns to white noise in my beleaguered exhausted brain.

"Could you take me there, please?" I ask.

"Of course, ma'am."

We begin our walk, heading for the stairs. "How're you enjoying your stay so far, ma'am?" There's a soft hint of sympathy in her voice. It seems she's been informed I'm here on a solo honeymoon.

I immediately squash any pity heading my way. "Everything is great. Could you tell me more about the history of the palace?" I majored in history in college, which has come in very useful for writing historical romance. Not sure that

Yale would like to take credit for contributing to my sexy romance novels, but hey, I appreciate the fine education.

Christina dutifully launches into the palace's history. Unfortunately, I'm too tired to process it all. I'm with her in the beginning with the Vikings, who sailed here with their Irish wives from an early Irish settlement and constructed a round stone fortress. She loses me somewhere along the second fire.

"We're here, ma'am," she says, stopping by a wooden door in a long hallway lined with windows. "The gardens are just past the courtyard." She points toward it through the window. It's a nice view of a grassy courtyard flanked by the east and west wings of the palace with manicured formal gardens in the distance.

"Thank you."

She bobs a curtsy and leaves. I open the door and step out into a sunny June day with clear blue skies and white fluffy clouds. I feel better already. I head to the center of the courtyard, throw my head back, spread my arms wide, and close my eyes. The sun warms my face. I don't need a groom to enjoy this. In fact, Mason would've probably preferred we spend our time cycling around the island. He was big into cycling. I could never get comfortable on that tiny bicycle seat. Welp, now I don't have to do what he wants to do. I'm a free woman. I straighten, a heaviness sinking into my limbs.

My phone rings, and I snatch it from my pocket, thankful for the distraction. My editor's name pops up on the screen. *Yes!* I punch the button. "I've got my next book."

"Let's hear it," Quinn says. She's a New Yorker—direct and to the point.

I take a seat on a nearby stone bench. "We've only seen glimpses of William before this in the other two books, so I'm going to give him a dark past. He's a scoundrel."

"Like it so far."

"It'll be a love triangle. A scoundrel and a slick gentleman both want the heroine. Her name will be Sigourney, which means victorious conqueror." I rush on because we both know Sigourney is not a Regency-era name, but I love that she's so kickass. "It's the slick gentleman she will make pay and use the scoundrel to ruin him. In the end, both men will be ruined." My heart beats a little faster, excited at the idea of crushing two men.

Silence.

"Quinn? Are you still there?"

"Yes," she says quietly. "How're you feeling?"

"I'm fine. What's wrong? You don't like it? It's exciting. She'll bring them to their knees."

"Maybe you're too bitter to write this story."

"I'm not too bitter!" My voice rises to an alarming pitch, and I lower it, working hard for a reasonable tone. "I'm fine. I have the story."

"This doesn't sound like an Alice Segal story. It's tragic."

My life is tragic. I swipe at an annoying tear and say urgently and loudly in an effort to convince her, "Dealing with a love triangle could be—"

"Give yourself a little more time to grieve," she says gently. "Send me something next week. Not ideas, an actual chapter. Better make it three, okay?" She mutters a quick goodbye and hangs up.

I stare at the phone in shock for a full minute. She didn't like my idea. That was my only idea. Three chapters by next week is generous. I should be turning in much more, but still.

Who am I kidding? I can't write romance when I don't believe in it. I'm *finished*. Career over.

I pull my knees up under my long dress like a turtle pulling into her shell. Then I wrap my arms around my knees, bury my head in my arms, and let the tears fall. I don't want to lose this author gig. I'm completely unemployable as a history major with no job experience. I went straight from college into writing. Maybe I'll end up teaching history to high school students, who don't give a crap about the past because they're too muddled with hormones and angst about where to sit in the lunchroom and who is their true friend and who is secretly talking about them behind their back. Not that I know anything about that.

This su-u-u-ucks donkey balls!

"Are you okay?" a deep male voice asks.

My head jerks up, and I stare in utter shock, the breath whooshing from my lungs. *Is it really him?* I take off my tear-splotched glasses, clean them with the end of my dress, and shove them back on for a better look. It is. Prince Lucas Rourke—the world's most eligible royal bachelor, the man who dates movie stars and models—is standing in front of me, asking if I'm okay. I suck in air. He's like a romance-novel cover. Truly. I wouldn't even need to write a story if I had him on the cover. People would buy my grocery list repeated a thousand times just to have his gorgeous self to gaze upon. His aquamarine eyes are a sharp contrast to his thick dark hair and neatly trimmed beard. If he were a hero in one of my stories, I'd describe him as six feet of broad-shouldered muscular perfection with a proud regal bearing. Maybe throw something in there about the snug fit of his breeches. Ahem. He's wearing a short-sleeved black button-down shirt, and his forearms are tanned and muscular. I'm a bit of a connoisseur of forearms, and his are particularly sexy. I can't help but notice this kind of thing. It's in my job description and does *not* mean I'm actually going to do anything about my appreciative admiration. My blackened heart prevents any blood flow south of the belly button.

I attempt a smile and manage to say, "I'm fine," which sounds unconvincing even to my ears. It was kind of him to check on me, but I'm not about to unload on a total stranger.

He shocks me further by taking a seat next to me on the bench. "I couldn't help but overhear about the love triangle. That sounds rough."

I don't know if I should laugh or cry because I was describing my story, and just now I realize I was describing my life. Duh. No wonder Quinn hated it. My life is far from a romance.

His aquamarine eyes are sympathetic. "You don't have to

talk about it. I'll just keep you company for a bit." And he stays put.

He's being there for me, a total stranger in the midst of a breakdown. I didn't even know he spent any time at the palace. I've seen pictures of him all over the world with many, many glamorous people, especially women. So many women. None of whom would ever be described as a curvy girl. What in the world is he doing here?

I risk a sideways glance at him without turning my head.

He offers a small smile. "I'm Lucas."

I snort. "I know who you are. You're the world's most eligible royal bachelor." His lips curve into a sexy crooked smile. "I'm Alice. I'm here on my honeymoon."

"Oh." He looks all around, probably wondering where the groom went. "I misunderstood. I thought you were a guest of my sister-in-law with your American accent." He looks back to me. "You must be in the honeymoon suite." At my nod, he lowers his voice. "Did you have a fight with your husband?"

"No. Well, yes." I flutter a hand in the air. "He's not here, and we're not married."

His brows knit. "Why did you say you were on your honeymoon?"

I hesitate, debating confiding in a stranger. I don't open up easily to anyone, and it's still so painful to talk about.

I lift my palms and force some energy into my voice. "I'm a badass." And then my chin quivers, completely destroying my credibility.

2

———————

Lucas

"Where are you from, badass?" I ask in an effort to hold off her tears.

"Portland, Oregon, USA," she says gamely and takes a deep quivering breath. She's trying not to lose it. I know the signs. You don't get to be the world's most eligible royal bachelor without having plenty of experience with women.

The contrast of her nerdy librarian glasses with her blond hair and lush curves caught my eye through the window a few moments ago. The breeze made her loose dress cling to her large breasts and hourglass figure. Incredibly sexy. Like if Marilyn Monroe wore nerdy glasses. It wasn't until I pushed the door open that I realized she was dealing with a crisis. Her voice, even in distress, is a smooth rich tone that's undeniably sexy. Why would she take a solo-honeymoon trip? The only thing I can think of is that it was paid for and she didn't want it to go to waste. A practical sort.

I check on the tears situation. None yet, though her blue eyes are shiny through her glasses. The black seriousness of the glasses is softened by little silver hearts on the corners of the frames. "So you'll be in the guest suite for a week?" I purposely avoid calling it the honeymoon suite under the circumstances.

"Two weeks."

I keep my voice upbeat like a two-week solo honeymoon could be a fun adventure. "Maybe you could do a little sightseeing in France. Nantes is close by, and Paris isn't too much farther. Of course, you could always tour Villroy, though there's not much to see beyond sand and sea."

She attempts to sound upbeat in return. "Yes, that was my plan. Just soak it all up, become inspired, and magically produce my next book." Her voice takes a downturn at the end there.

"What do you write?"

She sighs. "Historical romance. Love stories set in the Regency period in England. Well, I did. I may be fired soon." She slowly shakes her head. "My editor hated my love-triangle idea." She gives me a rueful smile. "It's also my real life."

"Sorry."

She shifts on the bench, tucking her legs under her, criss-crossed, and arranges her dress over her knees. "Enough about me. What are you up to? What does a prince do around the palace?"

"Actually, I've been involved with the business side of our new venture. We're building a day spa on the east side of the island and getting started with manufacturing cosmetics using local ingredients provided by the fishing industry." I love talking about the new business.

She brightens. "So you're also a businessman?"

Pride has me sitting a little straighter until I remember the difficulties I've had in proving myself worthy of the position. I'm the third-born son, which means I was never groomed for the throne or much of any royal duties beyond some photo ops. And I fully admit to being a freewheeling partier mixing it up with A-listers, but that's not all I am. I want to contribute to the kingdom, be part of the legacy. I should be the CEO of our new business venture. I have experience investing quite successfully in other start-up companies and serving on their advisory boards—angel investing being a hobby of mine—but here at home, I can't make headway. The king and queen—my oldest brother, Gabriel, and his wife, Anna—started us down this path and continue to oversee it, giving me very little to do despite my steadfast devotion to the business. They should be more concerned with running the country and not split their attention between the kingdom and business matters. Anna is due with their first child in two months and will be taking time off after that. Why not let me take the reins?

It's Gabriel who's the problem. He thwarts me at every turn. Half the time he jumps in for issues I said I would handle, and he's continually pulled away by his royal duties, which results in delayed decision-making and crews waiting on orders. If there were a clear role for me, a clear division of work, everything would run much more smoothly. It's so damn frustrating.

"Yes and no," I finally say. "I'm working on taking a greater role on the business side."

She looks off in the distance. "I wish I had practical skills like that. I'm not sure what I'm going to do now that my career is over."

"Why is your career over?"

She lifts one shoulder up and down. "I'm a writer and I can't write."

"Why not?"

She turns to me and says matter-of-factly, "Because Mason killed the muse." She looks straight ahead. "I don't believe in romance anymore, so I can't write it. I don't want to talk about it."

"Okay."

She slaps a hand on her thigh. "Screw Mason! Why does he get a happy-ever-after and I get to be alone on my honeymoon, looking at the dead carcass of my career?"

"So we are talking about it."

She shakes her head emphatically. "No. I'm not going

there. I'm not wasting my time rehashing what I've already wasted an entire week rehashing. I did the grief thing, the sobbing tear thing, the *how could you* thing; I'm done." She pushes her palm out in front of her. "I am moving on."

"That sounds health—"

"I mean, it's not like I want to marry him now, you know?" She jabs a finger in the air. "If he showed up right now, on his knees *begging* for forgiveness and showering me with chocolate and rose petals and diamonds, that would still be a hard no."

I almost laugh because chocolate came before diamonds in her mind, but she's scowling and clearly still in distress. "Tell me what happened."

She waves me off, her head turned away. "I don't want to unload on you. I just met you. No offense."

"Well, I am offended."

Her head whips toward me, her eyes wide. "You are?"

"Yes. You have a charming, handsome man sitting here ready to listen, and you're only giving part of the story. It's like a cliffhanger, and you, as an author, should know better than to leave the world's most eligible royal bachelor on the edge of his seat, not knowing the ending."

Her lips part as she stares at me. "I don't even know where to begin with what you just said. There's so much to unpack. The author swipe, the charming, handsome description of self, the fact that—"

"You don't think I'm charming and handsome?" I give her my crooked sexy smile that always works with women.

She flushes pink and tucks a lock of hair behind her ear. Even a woman in distress can't resist that smile.

"Well…" she says slowly as if she's being careful of what she says. She meets my eyes with a serious expression, and I'm struck by the sharp intelligence reflected there. "It was very kind of you to sit here with me while I have my existential crisis. It's just that some might say, not me but *some*, that referring to yourself as charming and handsome borders on the arrogant as opposed to someone else saying those things about you."

"Feel free to say them."

Her lips twist to the side, her blue eyes dancing with amusement. "You're charming and handsome."

"Thank you."

"And you know it."

I grin. "Everyone knows it, and you're smart and beautiful."

She gasps, her eyes wide.

"Why the shock?" I lean toward her ear, lowering my voice to a husky tone. "Surely you know that about yourself."

Bright pink dots her cheeks. Freaking adorable. She recovers herself and says, "Obviously I know that, but it's nice to hear you say it. Thank you."

I incline my head. "Now I sense Mason was the villain in this love triangle, but you tell me. Was it burn-his-picture bad or scorch-the-earth bad?" I sense more tears won't help her. She needs action, something cathartic.

She wrings her hands together. "Well, it wasn't the earth's fault. I guess it was burn-his-picture bad."

"Then let's do it. Do you have any pictures of him we could burn?"

"Only on my phone."

I wiggle my fingers for the phone. "Let me see."

"Why?"

I let out an exaggerated breath. "So we can put a hex on him of course. Next best thing to burning a picture."

"A royal businessman who performs witchcraft," she says as she pulls her phone out of a pocket in her dress. "Did *not* expect that. Probably an exorcism would work better though." She taps a few times, scrolls rapidly, and stares at the screen.

I pull her phone toward me. A tall skinny man with rumpled brown hair, round frameless glasses, and a prominent Adam's apple looks back at the camera rather smugly.

"He looks like a geek," I say, which is being polite. He looks like a smug ass, and I want to smack him already.

She turns her phone facedown on the bench. "He's an English professor at Spire College back in Oregon. We met at a bookstore."

"Still a geek."

"When he took off his glasses, it was a very Clark Kent-Superman kind of thing. He worked out. He was a catch, I promise you. Riley always said how lucky I was. That's my best friend." She stops abruptly. "*Was* my best friend. And now I guess she's the lucky one since they're in love." Her voice cracks, and she turns her head away.

There's the love triangle. I suspect the betrayal of her best friend is even worse than the betrayal of the smug ass. Women's friendships run deep. Damn, a double betrayal. No wonder she's a mess. She's keeping it together, but it's all right there just under the surface.

"What you need is to exorcise him," I say. "Start fresh." I'll leave the best-friend exorcism to another woman to fix. Maybe my sister-in-law, Anna. She's fiercely loyal to my mother and sisters. Woman power and all that good stuff. I don't know what exactly goes on with them, but they're tight.

She meets my gaze and says softly, "That's why I came here, but they *followed* me."

"We need to destroy something."

She straightens. "We do?"

"Absolutely. Okay, forget her. It's him we need to focus on. He's the one who broke your heart."

She sighs. "Riley's hard to forget. I knew her longer, since we were eleven when she defended me from a vicious bully. We were inseparable after that."

I wince. It just keeps getting worse. "That sounds horrific, but for now let's focus on exorcising your ex so you can enjoy your honeymoon more like a vacation. What reminds you of him?"

She lifts a finger to her cheek. "He had a dimple right—"

"No."

"And a cowlick." She smooths her hair with a wistful look. "It always stuck up a little in back."

Jesus. "Leaving out his betrayal, what else did you hate about him?"

She blinks up at me. "I didn't hate anything about him. I loved him." Still with the love after what this prick did? She's clearly not over him, and I'm angry on her behalf.

"So he was perfect. Nothing irritated you."

She looks at the sky and then says quietly, "He used to ask me when I was going to write something serious. He said my books were fluff." She lifts her chin. "My books are important to me. In fact, he never even read them. The first one won an award for debut novel; the second one made me a bestseller. His book never won an award or sold more than a couple of hundred copies."

I pounce on that. "He was jealous. Let's burn his book."

"Oh, I would never burn a book."

"I'm getting a hold of his no doubt pretentious book, and we're ripping off his geeky author photo from the back cover and burning it."

Her jaw drops, and she shuts it with a snap. "The book is called *Root in the Air*. It's a story about feeling like you have no roots because there's no longer a sense of community in the new generation of mobile commuters who follow the money."

Pretentious ass. "Let me guess, you read his book even though he never read yours."

"Yes, it was very well written."

"Did you like it?"

"Well, there were some good—"

"Did you like it?" I press.

"No. There was no story, really." She dances her fingers in the air. "It just wandered all over the place. Too many run-on sentences meant to be poetic. There were a lot of characters, a lot of different points of view, and they never added up to anything."

"Aha! Sounds like fluff."

She laughs, a musical delighted laugh that makes me smile. I did that. "Very serious highbrow fluff."

A sharp authoritative voice rings out through the courtyard. "There you are."

I snap to attention, getting to my feet. Hell. I was supposed to meet Gabriel to talk about an issue with construction on the spa and got distracted by Alice's problem. "I was just on my way."

He shakes his head from the open doorway. "It's taken care of. Feel free to continue flirting as usual."

"I wasn't...she was..." I trail off because he's already gone back inside, dismissing me.

I turn to Alice. "I need to go talk to my brother."

"Of course. Thanks for lending an ear." She picks up her phone and stares at the screen, at that stupid picture of her stupid ex.

I can't stand it. I snatch the phone out of her hands and tap over to her contacts, entering my number. Then I hand it back.

She gapes at me.

I don't know if she's surprised or offended by the presumption. "For the exorcism," I say before striding back inside.

I head in the direction Gabriel went, but he's already out of sight. I halt. He probably wouldn't hear me out anyway. He's convinced I'm not taking things seriously. What will it take to prove my commitment?

3

Lucas

I shift gears, heading toward the side exit, intending to drive down to the construction site and check on things myself. My phone vibrates with a text.

Testing. It's Alice.

Hope I didn't cause a problem for you with your brother.

Was that the king?

I stare at the screen, debating how much to say. I'm not supposed to discuss private matters with outsiders, even though my gut says to trust her, and I know she was vetted in advance if she's staying at the palace. I type a quick reply: *It's fine. Talk later.*

A few minutes later, I grab the keys to an old Renault in the service lot of the palace and drive down the long winding hill. Gabriel would insist I call for a driver to take me in one of the Mercedes with tinted windows, which would also send the signal for a guard to join me, but I can't be bothered. It's a short drive down to the construction site, and I've always felt safe on the island. The people here are used to me coming and going, and no one has ever intended harm toward me. Maybe some excited enthusiasm, especially by young women, but I've never minded that kind of attention. I love women.

I park in the gravelly lot next to the spa. We're two months into construction and should be finished in another six weeks. Unfortunately, we're behind schedule, not only because of the delay in decision-making from Gabriel's split attention, but also from weather-related delays in getting needed materials to the island and an unexpected shortage of float glass that Anna wanted for an array of windows facing the sea.

I open the glass door to the spa and step inside, grabbing a hard hat from a utility cart on my way to the reception area. There's a crew here now, putting up drywall. Gabriel and Anna are standing by the decorative water wall. He resembles me, same dark hair and blue-green eyes, same stature, but he's always clean-shaven. Anna is tall for a woman, only a few inches shorter than his six feet, with a mass of wild dark curls, brown eyes, and a heart-shaped face. She's unconventionally pretty, which suits her because she's also very unconventional in personality. It was quite a shake-up around here when Gabriel married her, an American commoner, making her queen. They're staring at the decorative wall, where a trickling waterfall is supposed to continuously run. It was working properly, briefly, before it began sporadically splashing onto the subfloor, which would damage it long term. It's shut off now.

As soon as I reach them, I say, "The technicians who installed the water wall aren't available for several weeks for repair. I can get a new one here—"

Gabriel cuts me off. "The problem is the pump. I've already ordered a new one from the manufacturer. One of our crew will install it."

"Okay, then," I say evenly, holding onto my temper. I said I would take care of it. He won't hand over control to me despite acknowledging that my ideas have merit. It's beyond frustrating. "Problem solved."

Anna smiles at me. "Hi, Lucas. Thanks for checking in."

I bite back what I really want to say. I've been doing a lot more than checking in around here. I've been living at the palace ever since we broke ground on construction back in early April, determined to contribute to the business. It's now June, so obviously I'm not going anywhere. This spa and the associated cosmetics line are the key to rescuing Villroy's faltering economy and ensuring we provide jobs that will keep the younger generation on the island. A kingdom made up only of the older generation will quickly die out. I refuse to let that happen. Villroy means everything to me.

I keep to a safe subject, one of Anna's favorites. "How are you feeling with the baby?"

She beams a bright smile and rubs a hand over her large baby bump. She's seven months pregnant. "Me and baby girl are great."

"Good."

Gabriel places his hand over her stomach. "Anna, let's go back to the palace. I don't like you here when there's still so much dust and construction activity."

She smiles, putting a hand to his jaw. He shifts his head, kissing her palm almost reverently before guiding her out, his hand on her lower back.

I follow them, feeling very much like a third wheel. That's been my experience with them with the business too. They're a united front rolling merrily along without me.

"It's really shaping up, isn't it?" Anna asks.

"Yes, at long last," Gabriel says.

"It's been a long expensive journey," I chime in. "Those construction delays were costly. Could we take a walk and talk a bit about finances?"

"Sure," Anna says, which prompts Gabriel to grumble his agreement. He's always amenable to her. Watching my brother go from his previous stuffy, grim, authoritative self to this new version of himself—a smiling, devoted husband—has been eye-opening. I never thought the love of a woman could change a person so much. It's certainly wasn't the case for me with my big relationship.

We exit the building and walk over to the far side of the flat area of land across from the spa. There's potential here for more construction, maybe a restaurant, but that's up in the air until the spa is earning enough to pay for itself.

I jump right in. "So what I'm thinking is we could raise some capital to take some of the heat off us. Everyone in the family contributed generously, but now it's getting to be a drain on our finances, and we still need to invest in manufacturing."

"It would be good to have an influx of capital," Gabriel says, "but we don't want to open up to outsiders. From the very beginning, this was our project. The Rourkes are behind the revitalization of Villroy. We have to be personally invested."

"And we are," I say patiently. "Everyone knows we put up the funds."

"Except for the contribution from my royal bachelor auction fundraiser," Anna adds with an impish smile. "Lucas really came through with us for that. My friends were wild to bid on you." Anna kick-started everything with the fundraiser, mostly to get her well-connected wealthy salon clients to feel invested in the spa so they'd return and spread the word to their friends. She used to be a beautician. Naturally, I was a much-sought-after bachelor, especially after I unbuttoned my shirt and teased at unbuttoning my trousers.

I grin. "Happy to help as always."

Anna smiles. "That was such fun. Unfortunately, we only raised enough to cover survey and engineering for the spa and research into the cosmetics line. This is a huge project." She turns to Gabriel. "Lucas is right. We're getting to the strain point, and we still need to tackle manufacturing."

Gabriel inclines his head. "I'm not saying he's not right; I'm saying we don't want outsiders."

I press on with my idea. "I'll take the lead on this. I'll look into banks for a loan. We'll pay it off, ultimately, and that way we don't have to give up any stake in the project. Outside investors would want a percentage equity."

"Do you think we could get favorable terms in this economy?" Anna asks.

"I do have a contact at a French bank who could be useful," Gabriel says.

"Perfect," I say. "Make me CEO. I'll take the proposal to them and have the authority to sign off on it."

"Anna and I are co-CEOs," Gabriel says.

I manage to speak civilly despite my frustration. This is not the first time we've had this conversation. "It's not written in stone anywhere. We need to run this more like a business and set up clearly defined responsibilities and roles. Right now it's too much like a family venture."

"It *is* a family venture," Gabriel says, the telltale ticking of the muscle in his jaw telling me he's nearly out of patience.

I press on. "If we want outside capital, the whole thing has to be professional and transparent. Dot the I's and cross the T's."

"There's no *I* or *T* in Lucas," Anna says with a smile. At my no doubt sour expression, she holds up a palm. "I'm not saying I disagree with you, but the fact is Gabriel and I are committed to each other and our life here together, which includes this business. You've spent the last ten years traveling. Gabriel says the last couple of months is the longest you've stayed on Villroy since you were a child."

"You doubt my commitment to Villroy?" I ask tightly. "I grew up here; my family is here. It is my home, my birthright, my legacy just as much as Gabriel's." Only I had the misfortune to be the third-born son as opposed to the first.

"What's keeping you here, Lucas?" she asks, not unkindly.

"I want to be in charge of this venture, put my stamp on it, and make a real contribution to the kingdom."

"Until the next beautiful woman turns your head," Gabriel puts in. "Then you're off with some starlet and you'll forget all about us." He refers to my ex, Nora, whom I briefly travelled with to movie locations.

I slam my hands on my hips. "What will it take to prove my commitment? A blood oath?"

"Maybe you could get engaged to a local woman," Anna says with a wink. "Then we know you're not going anywhere."

I cannot disguise my repulsion at the idea. Marriage is not for me. I enjoy my status as the most eligible royal bachelor. What I don't enjoy? Relationship drama. My ex and I put each other through the wringer with multiple fights, breakups, and reunions. It was exhausting, painful, and ultimately pointless.

She laughs. "Your face says it all. Anyway, I was joking. Marry for love and nothing less."

"I don't plan to marry at all."

"You never know," she says in a singsong voice.

"I know."

Gabriel crosses his arms. "This is just another reason Anna and I should retain control. If we go to a bank, our stability as a couple and as leaders of the kingdom will demonstrate our long-term commitment to the business."

I lift my palms. "So I guess I'm destined to be in the background."

"We appreciate you," Anna says.

"Yes, of course," Gabriel says. "When you're present and focused, you're a great help."

The backhanded compliment rankles. I bow my head to my king and queen. "I'll see you later. I'm heading over to the port to check on the tests." Small-scale testing for the cosmetics line is underway there. I leave before I can snap at them.

"Thanks, Lucas!" Anna calls as I walk away. "We appreciate you!"

It's the second time she's said so within the space of a few minutes, which only goes to show she knows how unappreciated I feel.

By the time I return to the palace, I realize I've been backed into a corner. If I give up my role here and leave the project to Gabriel and Anna, I've only proven Gabriel's point that I'm not committed to the business. If I stay, I'll be constantly thwarted by the lack of confidence and authority invested in me. How do I prove I'm committed to life here on Villroy? Maybe if I'm the one who brings in the money. But I don't even have the authority to sign off on a loan. Back to the corner for me.

If I were truly as unattached to Villroy as Gabriel says, I would've stayed with Nora. It's why we broke up. She wanted me to move around with her from movie location to location indefinitely, and after a few months in Canada and then California with her, I longed for home. Sure, I travel quite a bit, but Villroy is in my blood and I would never abandon her completely. Not for anyone. Maybe what Nora and I had was never really love. Sure, the sex was fantastic, but half the time we fought like cats and dogs. I always thought the fighting proved our love, there was such an intensity of feeling. Maybe I don't even know what love is.

Who the hell cares? I'm happy. I have everything I need, except my brother's faith in my abilities to run this project.

And that's the only thing I truly want.

4

Alice

I have two activities scheduled for tomorrow—a morning tour of the palace with the nice maid Christina, who helped me find my way earlier, and an afternoon tea with the king and queen in the parlor. After that, there are options for the rest of my two-week stay. I can arrange to have the royal yacht take me to France, or stay here and enjoy a picnic on the beach, or request a driver or a bicycle for touring the island. It's a very low-key honeymoon trip, which I had anticipated spending mostly in bed and then later decided in a fit of wild optimism I'd spend mostly writing. The likelihood of the latter is rapidly approaching zero.

I press a hand to my growling stomach. It's dinnertime, and I have a candlelit dinner in the formal dining room reserved for my first night on the island. The formal dining room is only used for special royal occasions. All part of the package—one dinner in the formal dining room, one audience with the king and queen. I consider taking dinner in my room due to the solo deal. *No. You're a badass, remember?* Staying in my room defeats the purpose of coming here. This is my *I can enjoy myself without you just fine* trip. While I'm not exactly looking forward to the reminder of my nonromantic solo honeymoon at a candlelit dinner, I do have to eat. Okay, that settles it.

I pull out my phone and text Lucas in another fit of wild optimism. Why not? He gave me his number. I don't know why. Maybe he's bored. Maybe he pities me in my solo-honeymoon state. I don't care. He reached out to me in a time of distress, and now I will reach out to him in a time of awkwardness.

Hi. It's Alice. Would you like to burn stuff, perform an exorcism, or join me for dinner?

Please choose two or more of the above.

Lucas did encourage me to burn stuff as a sort of exorcism of Mason's evil spirit. I stare at the screen for a moment, wondering if that was too forward. He's probably busy with royal duties, or maybe he's already jetted off the island to meet up with one of his many gorgeous girlfriends. I'm sure he's never wanting for company. Screw it. I'm going to my candlelit dinner and using it as book research. After all, there was plenty of candlelight back in Regency times, and I haven't personally experienced it very often. I call down to the servants' quarters to let them know I'll be down shortly for dinner.

Then I dress as befitting a special occasion. I did shop for my honeymoon, including sexy island-appropriate clothes, dressy outfits, and lingerie. I should burn the lingerie. I feel nearly evil at the thought of burning such pretty things. In any case, shopping for the honeymoon was just one of the many wedding things that distracted me from writing. I'd like to say I had my suspicions about Riley and Mason and that was what kept me from writing, but I was clueless until he told me. To be fair to my keen powers of observation and general intelligence, I trusted them both and there were no obvious signs. I later found out, through Mason's oh-so-helpful detailed explanation of how he realized he was *truly* in love with her, that they spent mornings together before she had to go to work (she worked a later shift due to being a chef), and late at night when he claimed to be at faculty events. They also spent a few weekends together when I thought he was visiting his brother in Wyoming. Whatever!

I. Will. Enjoy. Myself.

Even if I die a little inside with each reminder.

Here I go, dressing for the occasion in my new light blue maxi dress. Someone once told me this shade of blue brings out the blue in my eyes. I adjust the cute little off-the-shoulder sleeves and tie the belt loosely at the waist. There's a deep V in the front of the dress, showing off my ample cleavage, and a dip in the back as well. Sexy and romantic. I take a seat at the vanity to slip on metallic gold gladiator sandals with block heels that give me another inch in height. My shoulder-length hair takes little time since I typically wear my hair down and it's straight as a stick. I spend more time on my makeup just for the hell of it. Eyeliner, mascara, blush, and a rosy red lipstick. Then I slip my glasses on, the lenses magnifying my made-up eyes. I never did get the hang of contacts.

At the appointed time, Christina returns to escort me to the formal dining room. I can't help but wonder where the actual royals are dining tonight. I doubt they're all dying to eat with a paying guest.

Once there, Christina opens the dining room door for me. "Here it is, ma'am. Enjoy your meal."

I peek into the empty candlelit room at a long gleaming dark wood table with a lonely place set for one wa-a-ay down near the end. *Go on, you need to eat. Be the badass.*

"Thank you," I tell her and step inside.

I take some mental notes, focusing anywhere but the lonely place setting. There's an enormous arrangement of cheerful yellow and white flowers in the center of the table. That's nice. The candlelight from silver candelabras on either side of the floral arrangement is very dim, flattering to all (if there were anyone else here to observe), and extremely romantic. I instantly imagine a seduction scene, beginning with my couple feeding each other and ending with the heroine bent over the table, her gown bunched in the center of her back as the hero thrusts into her, bringing them both to the heights of ecstasy. I flush with heat. My imagination is just that good.

Well, that's reassuring. I've still got the romance-author touch, though it's not quite a story. I search along the wall for the light switch in the room. Turns out I can only take so much romance solo. There, that's better. Light from the overhead chandelier brightens up the space. Okay, research. The room is quite beautiful. There's wood paneling and, on closer look, this table is definitely an antique. My place setting is elaborate with the royal china, shiny polished silverware, and a crystal goblet. I snap a picture with my phone and swallow over the tightness in my throat. It's hard to be a badass.

Maybe I'll eat and read on my phone. I did download a travel guide to London. That's my next stop for a book signing. My publisher covered the airfare out here for the book signing, which is how I was able to afford the honeymoon. Yes, I paid for the honeymoon myself, using my advance for the book I've yet to write. Mason was still paying off his grad school loans and didn't have the funds. Or so he said. I'm not inclined to believe anything he told me at this point. I take my seat, pull out my phone, and freeze. There's a voicemail from Mason. I turn the phone off vibrate so I'll hear it next time and can decline the call right away. A text pops up.

Mason: *Where are you? I want to talk.*

Riley thinks you took the honeymoon trip by yourself. Did you?

My chest constricts like it always does when I think of them together. I swipe a shaky finger over the texts and delete them. Then I delete the voicemail too, not even bothering to listen to it. It takes a lot for me to open up enough to trust someone, and he betrayed that trust. So did Riley. The day after Mason called off the wedding, Riley showed up at my apartment, begging for forgiveness and hoping we could keep our friendship. Yeah, right! I told her I never wanted to speak to her again. Her betrayal cut even deeper than Mason's after twelve years of friendship. She texted me three times after she begged for forgiveness, urging me to call her.

Some sick part of me likes that she feels remorse. She should, and I hope it lingers like a festering wound. Who me, bitter?

I swear from this point on, I will only associate with one hundred percent honest people. I'll make new people in my life sign something, like a prenup (that covers friendship and lovers), before the relationship is official.

I drop my head in my hand. That's just sad. See what you two drove me to? I need an honesty contract to have any kind of relationship!

Another text pops up, and my heart beats a little faster. Lucas!

I've got you in my contacts now, so you don't need to say It's Alice every time. Burning stuff sounds good to me. Where are you?

Maybe I should just skip dinner and go straight to burning stuff. I'm not feeling the solo-dining experience anyway. I could always grab something to eat later. Just then a servant enters, an older man with thinning white hair. He's carrying a pitcher of water with lemon slices in it. I smile at him and text rapidly.

I'm in the formal dining room.

Lucas: *Who else is there?*

Me: *An elderly gentleman. He's pouring me some water.*

Lucas: *You're dining alone with the servants?*

That sounds about as lonely as I'm feeling. My thumbs fly over the keypad.

I'm thinking of leaving. This was the honeymoon dinner. It's fine. I only got to my glass of water.

Lucas: *Stay put. I'll join you.*

Oh! My stomach does a topsy-turvy flip. Oh my God, what if there was a picture of me and Lucas in the gossip rags and Mason and Riley saw it? #Badass #YouDidn'tBreak-MeLosers

I am, perhaps, slightly vengeful.

Ah, well, my imagination is getting away from me again. It's not like a gorgeous prince is after me. I invited him to join me for dinner earlier. I'm not into him beyond an appreciation for his kindness and his forearms. I'm off men, off relationships, all that jazz. Surely I can appreciate his romance-cover good looks without, um, any expectations. Certainly no forward moves on my part.

A PRINCE IS JOINING ME FOR DINNER IN THE FORMAL DINING ROOM!

Which is what I would text in all shouty caps to my former best friend, but instead it remains shouty in my head. Doesn't lessen the excitement of the event. In fact, it makes it worse having it all bottled up in my head with nowhere to go.

I pace the room, too jittery to stay in my seat.

"Ma'am, would you like your first course now?" the elderly gentleman asks.

"Actually, Prince Lucas will be joining me. Could you bring another place setting?"

He straightens abruptly. "Very good." He turns and leaves.

A few minutes later, there's another servant setting a place across from mine. Then another servant files in, standing at attention nearby, along with an intimidating man dressed in black with a wireless earpiece. Security?

Oh-kay. I smile at the servant standing at attention, and he gives me a small nod. I smile at security too, but he remains stone-faced.

"I'm harmless," I tell the security guy. "The only thing I kill is bugs, and I only do that if they enter my apartment. I just firmly believe they should stay in their natural habitat and out of mine." I'm babbling because it's really awkward to have security here as though I'm a risk to the prince's safety. Me, a danger? I cry at dog-food commercials. Anyone would after watching the puppy grow up, eating different lifestyle levels of dog food, and you just know he's going to die soon and his owner will be so sad. My empathy runs deep, which is what made me a good writer back in the day.

"No worries," I say to the guard in lieu of all that over-sharing.

"Yes, ma'am," he says, remaining alert and on guard.

Now there are two servants waiting at attention, the guard, and me. Feeling self-conscious, I take my seat. I consider pulling out my phone, but it suddenly seems out of place now that dinner is a more formal affair with the additional staff. So I sip water and fiddle with the edge of my cloth napkin and wait. Tick-tock, tick-tock. There's a lot of quiet people in this room waiting for the prince to arrive.

Awkward.

Finally, Lucas bursts into the room with a cheery, "I'm here! Let the party begin!"

A laugh bursts out of me. "Now it *is* a party." He took the time to dress nice for dinner with a black blazer over a white dress shirt and tailored black pants, so I forgive him for making me wait awkwardly with his staff and security. Not that I could ever be mad at such a kindhearted prince taking the time out of his busy schedule to keep me company during this difficult time. It gives me hope that my solo honeymoon will get easier by the day. I will soon truly be the badass.

He takes the seat across from me, requests his drink from the servant, who hovers over his shoulder, and turns to the guard. "Arthur, you can go. I know her."

Arthur is unmoved. "Sir, she arrived today. You do not know her."

Lucas remains firm. "She's been vetted by the queen before her arrival, and I've already spent some time with her. Alice has been through an ordeal, and our conversation will be of a delicate nature. Please give us our privacy."

So aptly put. That's exactly what it was—an ordeal. I will refer to the Mason-Riley mess as the Ordeal from now on. It's the perfect descriptor and it packages it up nicely for eventually putting the Ordeal behind me. You can move away from a capital-letter object much easier than untangling from two complicated relationships with actual people.

Arthur bows his head. "I will be just outside the room, Your Highness."

"Not necessary, but fine," Lucas replies.

The moment the guard leaves, Lucas leans across the table and whispers, "Sorry about that."

"It's no problem. Thanks for joining me for dinner. I was starting to have second thoughts, though I confess eating in my room felt a little too much like giving up."

"You're a fighter. I admire that."

My cheeks heat. "I never thought of myself as a fighter before." I've always felt rather gentle, embracing the sweeter side of life. Granted, most of that sweetness is in my imagination, but I like spending time there. It's that rosy outlook that helps me write such life-affirming stories.

One corner of his mouth kicks up. "Maybe *fighter* isn't the right word. You're strong. Only a strong woman would dare take her honeymoon trip after what you've been through."

I blink back the sting of tears. "Yes, well, I'd rather not dwell on that."

"Right."

My phone rings, and I jump. I quickly decline the call and set the phone to vibrate. Mason again. What could he possibly want with me? Leave me alone! Another text pops up from him.

You can't avoid me forever. Please call me back. It's important.

I clench my teeth and meet Lucas's curious eyes. "It's my ex being rather insistent."

"Is he harassing you?"

"I don't know what he wants. He keeps saying we need to talk. Oh, crap. Do you think something happened? Maybe he's in the hospital gravely injured." I don't want to be with him, but I don't want him dead. I was deeply in love with him for a year. Gah, this is why I need an honesty contract from here on out. My natural empathy makes my heart too vulnerable.

"Then let his girlfriend take care of him," Lucas says, an edge to his voice.

"Right," I murmur. But what if there was a fire or a devastating car accident or he's contracted some kind of disease that's highly infectious and I could experience symptoms at any moment? Like that monkey disease that eats your brain and makes you bonkers! I saw it in a movie once. My imagination can be an evil thing, filling in the blanks with worst-case scenarios.

"You're not still in love with him, are you?" Lucas asks.

"No way!"

He shakes his head.

"I'm not. Are you kidding me? I was momentarily worried and now I'm not."

He gives me a skeptical look.

"Moving on," I say brightly, turning off my phone.

A servant steps forward and speaks quietly to Lucas, who responds with a low conversation. After the servant leaves, Lucas says, "I just told him we'd take whatever the chef already had planned for your dinner. It's summer salad, lobster, and chocolate soufflé with cherry sauce. Hope that sounds good to you."

"It does!" My spirits lift. Dinner sounds wonderful, Mason and Riley can't reach me with my phone off, and now that I have company, I don't feel nearly so…well, pathetic.

A few minutes later, we're served two flutes of champagne. Suddenly it does feel like a party.

Lucas offers his glass in a toast. "To burning stuff."

I clink my glass against his. "Yes!" I take a sip, the bubbles and sweet taste making me positively cheerful.

"I didn't have time to pick up the smug ass's book, so what should we burn?"

"I was thinking my lingerie. Like, too bad you'll never get to see me in this! It was all brand-new stuff bought for the honeymoon."

He cocks his head. "You sure? Maybe you could wear it for a different guy."

I swipe a hand through the air. "No way. I've sworn off men forever."

He smirks and takes a sip of champagne.

"What? You don't believe me?"

"No."

"It's true." I take another healthy swallow of champagne. "I no longer believe in happy-ever-after." That makes me so sad, I guzzle the remainder of the champagne. A servant instantly steps forward and refills it.

Lucas leans back in his seat. "Everyone says that after a breakup. Two weeks later—"

"Two weeks! Is that what you do? Because I'm thinking more like years."

He lifts a hand lazily. "Okay."

Clearly he doesn't believe me. "Have you ever had a serious breakup?"

"Yes." He taps the table. "And the best way to get over someone is to get another someone under you. Or for you, another someone over you, whatever works for you."

My jaw drops. "I can't believe you just said that."

He lifts one shoulder in a careless shrug. "Just being honest."

"Pig." I slap a hand over my mouth. "That slipped out."

He gives me a cocky grin. "No, it didn't. You meant it. I don't apologize for enjoying myself. But, hey, if you want to burn your lingerie, we'll burn your lingerie."

"What do you burn after a breakup?"

"I don't generally keep anything, so there's nothing to burn."

"Nothing?" I press. "Not even a left-behind shirt or a love note?" Mason penned some poetry for me.

"Oh my Lord, she has love notes." He leans back in his seat. "Let me guess, they were poorly written poetry."

"They weren't that bad." I hate to admit I was thrilled to get them. It seemed exceedingly romantic, and no man had ever written me anything beyond a text before that.

"I hope you burned them."

I bite back a smile. It's so nice to have such a staunch supporter. "Close. I put them in the shredder. They're confetti."

"Too bad you don't have them here because we could throw that on the fire too."

"It is too bad."

The first course arrives, salad for both of us with fresh calamari on top of it. Not fried either. I can see the little suction cups on the tentacles. Gross.

Lucas digs into his with gusto.

I shift the tentacles to the side with my fork and try not to look at them.

"What's wrong?" he asks. "You don't like squid?"

"It just looks so alive and rubbery."

He lifts a tentacle, wiggles it around, and pops it in his mouth, chewing with a devilish grin.

I make a face. "Eww."

"Just try one," he says, leaning across the table, stabbing one of mine with a fork, and offering it up to me, making it wiggle like it's alive.

I clamp my lips shut and turn my head away.

He barks out a laugh. "You're missing out. It's fresh and delicious. Seafood is our major export."

I keep my eyes on my lettuce. "Yes, well, I'll just keep my tentacles exported to the far end of my plate."

He laughs. "So tell me more about what you write. You said Regency-period stories. When is that?"

I'm momentarily speechless. Men never want to hear about my work. I recover myself. "The Regency period of England was from eighteen eleven to eighteen twenty, and it was delightful for the upper class, what they call the *ton*. That's who I write about, dukes and viscounts and such. Anyway, that time was full of social events—balls and teas are my favorite—along with the fashion, lots of gowns and formal wear." I sigh happily. "It was a more genteel time."

"You should've stayed in a castle in England," he says. "What made you want to stay here?"

My cheeks heat, and I force a casual breezy tone. "I have a book signing in London in two weeks, and it's not that far from here. Combining the two trips made sense because the publisher paid for my airfare, which made the whole thing possible."

He studies me for a moment. "Still odd that you wanted to stay here and not England, considering what you write. How did you hear of us?"

I consider saying I read about Villroy in a bridal magazine, which I did, but my fascination with the island began before that. In any case, the coverage of the weddings held here didn't exactly make it sound like a dream destination. There was some hilarious mix-up of a double-booked wedding, including one featuring furries, people in stuffed animal suits. Probably a touchy subject. I go with the truth, though it makes me sound slightly stalkerish, which is the whole reason I'm embarrassed to admit why I'm here. But I do confess because honesty is important.

"I went to Yale with your sister Silvia."

"You did? Were you friends?"

I set my fork down. "No. She was a year ahead of me and, you know, she's a princess. She was up here, you know?" I lift my hand above my head.

"Is that where I am?" he asks in a teasing voice.

"You were up there oh so briefly."

"Ha!"

I grin. "Anyway, I saw her around campus, everyone knew who she was, and I admit I became fascinated with Villroy. I did some research into the island and thought it would be a nice place to visit. I hope that doesn't seem Silvia stalkerish. I didn't expect to see her here. Anyway, I heard she married Cade and settled in the US."

A servant steps forward and clears Lucas's salad plate. I nod and he takes mine as well.

"She did," Lucas says in regard to Silvia. "So what did you learn about Villroy?"

"Tons, actually. I'm a history buff. I read all about the various people who laid claim to the island as well as your traditional fishing way of life, which is still around, but dying out. That's why Villroy is branching into new industries."

His shoulders draw back as he says with obvious pride, "The rightful family has been in charge for the past couple of centuries. The Rourkes are descended from the original Viking tribe."

"The Wild Ones." I can't help my smile. What a great name for a renegade tribe. "Is that why you and your brothers are known for being a little bit wild?"

He tilts his head. "Little bit? I'm all the way wild."

I laugh. "Still quite the globe-trotting bachelor leaving a trail of broken hearts. I've seen your picture everywhere. It must be exhausting to keep up such a wild rep."

He studies his drink, his expression drawn, and I fear I said the wrong thing. *Oh no.* I feel wretched after he's been so kind.

"Lucas, I was just teasing. I'm sure you do serious work here too. You said you were assisting with the new business venture, right?"

He blows out a breath and meets my eyes. "Trying."

A servant returns with a platter with two bowls. A cold melon soup is set in front of me. I suppose it's a palate cleanser. I take a spoonful, enjoying the light flavor. I look up and notice Lucas isn't eating. "What's wrong? The business isn't going well?"

He rubs the back of his neck. "It's frustrating is all. I suppose my globe-trotting bachelor ways are biting me in the ass. I'm not given the authority or responsibilities I want because *some* think I'm not committed enough to the business to be trusted with them."

I fill in the blank over who the *some* are. Only the king and queen are above him, and there's been lots of press featuring their active involvement in the new business. "So how can you prove your commitment?"

"I don't know, time? It's already been a couple of months, but by the time I prove my commitment, there won't be anything left to do. I just want to contribute, to put my stamp on things." He shakes his head, his lips pinched together. "Forget I said all that. I'm not supposed to share private matters."

I wave it off with a flourish. "Consider it forgotten."

"Thanks." He takes a spoonful of soup. "What else is on your agenda? Doing anything fun tomorrow?"

For a brief moment I think he wants to do something with me, and I get a little thrill at the thought of being his friend and confidante, he's certainly been that for me, but then I realize he's just changing the subject. "I'm taking a tour of the palace, and in the afternoon I'm having tea with the king and queen."

He stiffens. "You are? I didn't know guests would be having an audience with the king and queen."

"Yes, it's one of the perks of staying here. Just the one meeting."

He mutters a curse under his breath. "Do not breathe a word of what I just told you to them."

"I swear I won't."

He grimaces, probably regretting sharing with me.

"It's really okay. I'll probably be too nervous to say more than two words to them."

One corner of his mouth curls up in a slow crooked smile. I swear he could get away with stealing an old lady's last loaf of bread with that ~~endearing~~ super-sexy smile. (Writer hazard, I edit my own thoughts.) The man radiates sexual confidence.

His voice is silky. "You don't have a problem saying more than two words to me."

I flush hot. "That's true, probably because you came to my rescue today on more than one depressing occasion." I shake off the gloomy reminder, determined to enjoy the here and now. "I'm normally a hard-core introvert. Riley is the one..." I trail off, a lump of emotion lodged in my throat. Riley is the one who laughed at my quietly muttered jokes that no one ever heard. I take a sip of water before saying, "I suppose you made me feel comfortable with your kindness."

He gives me a cocky grin. "That's why they call me a charmer."

"And so modest too." I'm actually smiling, a real

delighted smile. After the Ordeal, the solo honeymoon, the writer's block, Lucas has resurrected my smile.

"I've never been accused of that sin."

I lean in. "What sins are you guilty of?"

"I don't trouble myself with guilt."

I lift my brows, waiting for an answer.

He grins, leaning in. "Too many to count. I'm the worst."

I laugh. "I think I'd like to be the worst too. It sounds fun."

He lifts a palm. "Glad I could be such a positive influence."

Lucas

Dinner with Alice was more relaxed than I thought it'd be. I anticipated she'd be in a sorry state like she was when I saw her earlier, but she's resilient and strong. I can't help but admire that, especially after learning the scope of the betrayal. Her fiancé and her best friend hooking up? That's like one of those tearjerker movies my ex was into. She would ugly cry over those pretend people. Alice is dealing with it for real. Rather well, I think, too, though I couldn't help but notice her ex is still in touch with her, and she seems like she's considering keeping the connection. Me? I would never look back. I've always been a realist. Alice is a romantic. She'd have to be to write love stories.

Now I'm waiting in the living room of the guest suite while Alice gathers up the lingerie she wants to burn. I've got matches and the keys to the storage chest, where we keep the firepit and assorted tools, in my pocket. This suite was meant to be what guests imagine royal life to be like, and it's suitably over the top with a fantastical ceiling mural, glowing columns, cherubs, even sconces meant to look like candles. My own suite is simple elegance—leather club chairs in the living room, antique mahogany furniture in the bedroom, nothing fussy or too gilded.

She emerges with a large black faux leather purse over one shoulder. "Okay, it's all here. Are we burning it in a fireplace or somewhere outdoors?"

"We'll make a fire on the beach. There's a metal firepit we use on occasion."

"Cool. Should I bring a jacket?"

I take in her dress, which exposes her smooth bare shoulders and her fantastic swell of cleavage, and think it a shame to cover it all. No, I'm not about to seduce a vulnerable woman who just got dumped by her fiancé. I'm not a total lech, and that is a situation ripe for the kind of drama I avoid like the plague. I just like looking at her. A lot. Unlike the women I usually date, who work with personal trainers for their sleek toned bodies, Alice looks soft, rounded with curves. *Lush* is the only word that seems to fit. Lush with curves, very feminine, and she smells like flowers.

I'm wearing a blazer over my white dress shirt since we dress for dinner in the formal dining room. "I'll give you my blazer if you get cold."

Pink colors her cheeks. "What a princely gesture."

I lift my palms. "Did you expect anything less?"

Her blue eyes sparkle through her cat's-eye glasses as she smiles. I get a thrill of triumph every time I make her smile, knowing the troubled place she's in right now. "You live up to the princely hype," she declares.

I make a formal bow before gesturing to the door. "Shall we?"

"We shall."

She brushes past me and wobbles a bit. I catch her by the elbow, steadying her. She looks up at me, her eyes bright, her voice a little breathy. "Thanks. I'm not used to these heels."

There's something unique in her eyes, something I don't often see, a gentle vulnerability lurking under that strong resiliency. I have the strangest urge to shield her from the harshness of life. Some primal inner-caveman thing going on here. Where did that come from?

She looks pointedly at my hand still gripping her by the

elbow, only somehow my fingers have splayed further, touching her soft satiny skin.

I shake my head, returning to reality, and drop my hold on her. "Off we go."

As soon as we leave the room, Arthur, the palace guard, trails us from where he's been waiting in the hallway. He trusts no one. It's his job, I know, but what Alice and I are about to do is a cathartic experience. She won't be able to get angry and let go with witnesses.

"Just a minute," I tell Alice before going to Arthur. "You're officially off duty," I tell him. "By my command."

He bows his head and takes his leave.

I join Alice a moment later. She gives me a sideways look as we walk down the hall. "Just the two of us, then, huh?"

"I thought you might like some privacy."

She looks straight ahead. "Right. Lingerie."

"Not because of what we're burning. Because of the cathartic element. You may cry or rage or dance on the ashes, I don't know. I wanted to give you the freedom to do what you need to do."

She halts, staring at me with a slack jaw.

"What?"

She shuts her jaw and tilts her head. "You're uncommonly in tune to a woman's emotional needs."

The tips of my ears burn, and I resume walking. Did she just call me sensitive? Every manly bone in my body protests. "I have *plenty* of experience with women."

"And I have plenty of experience with men."

I nearly trip. "You do?"

"How's it sound coming out of my mouth?"

"Shocking."

"It sounds like bragging coming out of your mouth."

"Touché."

"It's not your fault," she says matter-of-factly as we head downstairs. "It's the double standard. Men can prowl. Women are supposed to be choosy. But who are the men prowling with if the women are choosy?"

Fascinated, I can't help but ask, "Do you really have a lot of experience?"

She huffs and rolls her eyes.

"What?"

"Why does it matter?" she asks belligerently.

I lift one shoulder. "I don't know. You seem young. You said you were a year younger than Silvia, so I was just curious."

She brushes me away with a flick of her hand. "First, you. You're, what, thirty and—"

"I'm twenty-nine," I fire back. "Just turned it last week."

"Ooh, touchy. Hanging on to our twenties, are we?"

"No. I don't care. It's just a question of accuracy."

"Uh-huh."

"It is," I insist, though even I hear the defensiveness in my voice. I'm getting older, and the fact is, I feel it. I don't want to travel so much. And now that there's an opportunity for me to contribute to the kingdom, I want to settle down here on Villroy and make my mark. Yet all people see is how I used to be—the globe-trotting party guy.

"So you've been with a hundred women, give or take?" she asks.

"I never counted."

"Lost track?"

"I'm not that bad." I lead the way, heading for the courtyard. "Yes, I've enjoyed women. Yes, I have experience. I got serious once, so I'm capable of a relationship." I shove a hand in my hair. "Why're we even talking about this?"

"Touchy, touchy, touchy." She points at me with a small knowing smile. "You, sir, are a scoundrel."

I bark out a laugh. "Okay. And what are you?"

"A happy spinster."

"Somehow we were just transported to Regency England."

"I live there most of the time," she says cheerfully.

"Does that mean you aren't so experienced with men?"

"I know men, trust me."

"Do you now? What do you know?" I'm expecting her to declare all men are pigs, myself included. She did call me that at dinner, but she surprises me yet again.

She taps her temple. "I know how they think. Just ask any of my readers. I believably capture the male point of view."

I halt. "Wait. Are you telling me your experience with men is solely an intellectual exercise?"

"No!" Her cheeks flush bright pink.

Is she embarrassed over her lack of experience? That's easily remedied. Any man would want her, and it's not terribly difficult to get a guy to sleep with a sexy woman.

A gentleman would let it drop. I really am a scoundrel. "Well, you just said to ask your readers."

She pulls out a pink lacy scrap from her purse. "Would an inexperienced woman own this?"

My mouth goes dry. It's a lace and mesh chemise with half cups that would likely push up her ample breasts. It's sheer in so many places, and my imagination fills in soft smooth skin, the curve of her hip, and lower. Skinny straps hang from the bottom of the chemise, meant to clip onto thigh-high stockings, probably sheer white. I can see it all much too vividly. Sweat breaks out on my forehead.

She shoves it back in her purse. "I thought not," she says smugly.

I keep walking, trying to think of anything but that sexy lingerie. I can't act on this attraction. I outline the reasons in my mind—

This is a vulnerable woman in need of a shoulder to cry on.

She is a temporary guest here.

She just swore off men.

Her ex isn't quite out of the picture.

Even knowing all this, my cock rises to the occasion. Hell. I truly am the worst.

5

―――――

Alice

I follow Lucas through the palace courtyard, enjoying the tickle of grass on the sides of my feet. "Hold on. I'm going to take off my sandals." I wobble as I try to balance on one foot, and he holds me firmly by the upper arm, steadying me. Warmth spreads from the spot where his large hand meets my bare arm. I ignore it. A biological reaction to skin on skin, maybe a chemical reaction. I don't know. I'm not sciencey. Why won't this stupid sandal come off? The strap is too tight. I need to unbuckle it. I give myself a stern talking-to about being here to heal, not to notice chemical reactions to people who are simply helping me. I grunt in frustration as my fingers fumble to set my foot free.

"Need some assistance?" he asks.

"No, I got it," I say through my teeth. The last thing I want is his hands on another part of my body. I can only ignore so much heat.

"Let me," he says. "It's the buckle, right?"

"I got it." Finally, my foot is free. Now for the other. *Come on!* This shouldn't be so hard. Heat flushes my cheeks, only now it's because I desperately need to put some space between us. He smells amazing. And that does *not* matter.

There is no way someone like him—a gorgeous prince who dates models and movie stars—could ever be interested in a plain nerdy girl like me. And I'm not interested in starting something anyway. I've got baggage that reaches across the Atlantic, across the entire US, and back to Oregon. So much frigging baggage it would crush any man in my vicinity. And I'm sure Lucas comes with his own baggage. Everyone does, and I can't deal with all that. I really can't.

Mercifully, the sandal cooperates, and I'm finally barefoot in the grass. I continue our walk, keeping my mouth shut so I don't babble something inappropriate that gives away my errant thoughts. Lucas is quiet too. I can't help but imagine what he might be thinking. It's a writer hazard that I invent dialogue, spoken or internal, for the people around me.

Lucas (secret thoughts): *This woman is a hot mess. So out of sorts over the Ordeal she can't even remove her own sandal.*

Confident Alice (retaliating telepathically): *You try removing a sandal while the hottest man you've ever met is touching your arm (substitute woman for yourself) and suddenly rebound sex is sounding like a fantastic idea.*

Alice (spoken in shock and longing as he leans kissing close): *"Wh-what're you doing?"*

I grit my teeth. Stop the madness!

My God, I have a sick mind. All that from his hand on my arm. I need to get a grip on reality. I *am* a hot mess, and Lucas wouldn't be interested in me even if I wasn't. Hello! He's the world's most eligible royal bachelor. He could have anyone, and his preference, as anyone who's ever seen a tabloid, TV, magazine, or the internet knows, is always a glamorous woman. Sometimes he branches out from superhot actresses to superhot models, but he does *not* seek out abundantly curvy, nerdy authors.

Rebound sex. *Right, Alice, like you would ever.* I have never been a casual-sex kind of person. At least not on purpose. It was the guy running out the door that made it so. I stifle a sigh. My romantic expectations have so rarely been met.

A few minutes later, we're past the courtyard, heading

into the formal gardens. It's so breathtaking I stop trying to talk myself out of my attraction to Lucas. The gardens are shaped by box hedges in straight lines with manicured trees, some of them perfectly round, others a wavy shape. Four long terraces of grassy slopes lead down to the sea. The moon is nearly full and lends a romantic glow over everything. Too bad I'm here to burn romance. Badass priorities.

"I have to come back here in the daytime," I tell him. "It's gorgeous."

"You should. The staff go to a lot of effort to maintain the gardens. Of course, when we were kids, we didn't appreciate that. We wanted a shrubbery maze instead."

I laugh. "That would be fun too." A marble fountain of fish spouting water in crisscrossing arcs comes into view. "Cute fountain!"

"One of my mother's rare touches of whimsy. She added it when she first arrived on Villroy as a new bride."

"I love it. It's playful. Is that how she is?"

"Oh-hh no. Not at all. Though, in her defense, she was the queen and mother to seven children, five of whom were unruly boys. My sisters were much more proper rule followers."

"Maybe now that you're all grown, she can find that playfulness within her again."

He gives me a sideways look. "Bit of an optimist, eh?"

"Of course. I have to be. My stories always end happily. I mean, back when I was writing them. Now—"

"You will again. You just need to let go of some of the rubbish mucking up the works."

I nod. "I sincerely hope you're right."

"Of course I'm right. You'll learn I'm always right."

"There's that modesty again."

His crooked sexy smile emerges, making it hard to find fault with any arrogant thing that comes out of his mouth. "I fear modesty isn't in my DNA. If you met my brothers, you'd understand. We're the same that way."

"Tomorrow I'll meet Gabriel."

"Ah. He's the exception to the charming thing the rest of us have going on. Very serious." He glowers impressively, his brows drawn together, his lips in a flat line. "Though he's mellowed considerably since he married Anna."

"I suppose having the weight of the kingdom on your shoulders could make anyone serious. It's a heavy responsibility."

He frowns and snaps, "Which is all the more reason he should delegate the business responsibilities to me."

I blink, momentarily startled by the unexpected harsh tone from such a laid-back guy.

He turns, muttering as he walks away, "I'll go fetch the firepit."

I continue on, reaching the beach, my feet squishing into the soft silky sand. Something in me relaxes. It's almost like I traveled all this way for this moment. Soft sand between my toes, the soothing waves, the glow of moonlight overhead. It's like something out of one of my stories, only it's real. I keep going, drawn by the hypnotic pull of the sea. The sand turns wet, cooler, and I go farther in, letting the baby waves run over my feet, feeling the pull of the undertow as it draws back. A deep sense of contentment fills me. All of my thoughts, my constant internal chatter, quiet down, and for the first time in a week I'm truly at peace.

A few relaxing minutes later, Lucas calls from behind me, "Got the firepit."

I turn to see him carrying a metal bowl that resembles a Viking shield. "That looks heavy."

"It's solid steel. Of course it's heavy."

"I don't need to burn the lingerie."

He halts. "You don't?"

"No, just being here with the water has helped a lot."

He lifts the firepit higher in the air, displaying impressive upper-body strength. "What am I supposed to burn, then?"

"Put the firepit back and stand in the waves with me. It's so relaxing."

He grumbles and heads back to the storage chest, an old

metal thing partially hidden behind a short white fence and a dune.

I tuck my glasses into my purse and set my stuff on the dry sand before returning to the sea. I'm nearsighted, so the whole scene takes on a muted glow. It's a private beach, and we're the only ones here. I look up, stargazing, feeling the dreamy state I used to feel before my world caved in on me. I spend a lot of time in my head, and it's normally peaceful there. After a few moments, I venture deeper into the water, enjoying the splash of waves around my ankles. I turn to see a blurry Lucas shedding his blazer, then his shoes and socks, setting them in a neat pile on the sand before rolling up the cuffs of his pants.

He joins me a moment later and winces when the water hits his feet. "It's cold! What're you doing in it up to your ankles?"

"It's refreshing!"

He turns. "I'm going back on the sand."

I scoop up some water and splash him in the back with it. He yelps, and I laugh. He turns, scoops up a huge handful of water, and splashes me in the face. I sputter, tasting salt in my mouth, shove the hair out of my face, and splash him like crazy, using both my hands and feet, kicking up water. He retaliates, and it's an all-out splash war. I can't stop laughing.

He leaps away. "Okay! Truce! I'm soaked!"

I look down at myself, my dress nearly translucent as it clings to me. "So am I!"

He stares at my dress, lingering on my breasts, as all men do, before jerking his gaze back to my eyes. His voice is hoarse. "You're a bad influence."

"Why, thank you. That's a first for me."

"Come on. Out of the water." He gestures for me to join him, backing up a step, but I'm not sure if I trust him not to splash me if I get closer. I suspect he's sneaky that way.

I hold out my palm, holding him off as I skirt around him and back to the sand. A light breeze chills me, and I shiver.

Lucas picks up his blazer, shakes it out, and then places it over my shoulders. The gesture surprises me, though he did offer it earlier. It's just that we're both soaked, and I imagine he's just as cold as I am.

"Thank you," I say softly, overwhelmed by the beautifully romantic gesture. Scratch that. Beautifully *caring like a wonderful friend* gesture.

He gazes into my eyes, serious now, his voice gruff. "You look different without your glasses."

"Thanks?" I'm not sure if different means good or weird. I always thought my glasses were cute.

He turns away. "We should go back." He scoops up his things and hands me my purse.

I slip my glasses on and follow him back toward the palace, relaxed and happy. I never thought I'd even get close to happy on this trip. I'd planned to soldier through, do my work, and make the best of it. I have the sudden urge to hug him for making my experience here so much more bearable. I can't, though. We don't know each other well enough for that, and I know it's improper to touch a royal without them initiating it, even if it's meant affectionately.

He turns to me. "Sure you don't want to get angry and destroy stuff?"

I shake my head. "I don't know if it's the sea, the island, or..." I don't want to say "you" because it sounds like I'm interested in him, which I'm not. I'm *appreciative* of him.

"Or what?" he asks.

I smile, truly grateful for his company today. "Or your friendliness, but I feel very relaxed. Like I was able to let go of some of that angst I was hanging onto. Believe me, I did my share of tears and anger back home, a pretty twenty-four-seven thing, but now, I don't know, something in me shifted." I halt, suddenly serious because I'm feeling close to him. "If you could just swear never to lie to me, to be one hundred percent honest at all times, then we can officially be friends."

He cocks his head. "I have to take an oath to be your friend? The blazer isn't enough? I'm chilled to the bone, you know." He crosses his arms and fakes a shiver.

I laugh a little. "I know I sound crazy, but I have been through *hell*. And I need some assurance. Can I trust you? Are you a man of honor?" My fictional heroes are men of honor, but I've met very few in real life.

He gets serious, his gaze intent on mine. "I swear on my life, Alice. I am a man of honor."

I let out a breath. "Thank you. And I promise to always be honest with you in return. I'm so glad you're my friend. I really need one right now."

He makes a formal bow. "Just another of my princely services."

I attempt a curtsy in my soaked dress. "Much obliged, Your Highness."

Our eyes lock as I straighten, the air shimmering between us with a charge of awareness. My breath stalls, my knees suddenly wobbly. It's elemental—man and woman meeting on a primal level. A hot shiver courses through me. I write about these moments. I have never in my life experienced one.

He shakes his head, blinking a few times before saying, "You're cold. Let's go back inside."

6

____

Alice

My maid, Christina, escorts me to the parlor for tea with the king and queen the next afternoon. I keep telling myself they're just regular people, young too, so it's not like they'll be dour and overly proper, but I can't seem to shake my nerves. I know to bow my head, curtsy, and call them Your Majesty or Your Majesties to address them together. After that, I'm at a loss. I'm terrible at small talk. I *so* want this not to be awkward. I was actually looking forward to it back when I thought I'd be here with you-know-who before the Ordeal. I do better conversation-wise with a little backup.

The door shuts behind me, and I'm alone in the parlor. It's a bright room with a wall of windows, along with a gleaming wood table and antique-looking wooden dining chairs with deep red velvet cushioned seats. In the center of the table sits a large fruit bowl with real fruit, not the fake stuff people use as a decoration. A small seating area with four high-back upholstered chairs and a round table is set off to one side. I'm not sure if I should sit at the big table or in the seating area.

I wipe my clammy hands down my sides and walk to the window, admiring the view in the distance of rugged cliffs with inlets of sandy beach. I decide standing is my best bet and the easiest way to drop into a proper curtsy. I smooth the pleated folds of my navy blue A-line dress. It's super cute with a simple short-sleeved bodice that cinches at the waist, and there's pockets. Now I have something to do with my hands. I accessorized with a chunky blue and gold necklace, and I'm wearing new black wedge heels with embroidered flowers.

I stick my hands in my pockets and make a slow stroll around the room, working hard to stay calm. A few moments later, the door opens suddenly and my heart races, but it's just a servant pushing a cart with the tea service over to the small seating area. "Hi."

He glances over at me. "Good afternoon, ma'am. The queen will be here shortly."

I bob my head. "Good. Okay. Thanks." I scratch the side of my neck. "Good afternoon to you too."

He leaves with a bow of his head.

I wait, staring at the delicious-looking three-tiered platter of tiny sandwiches, mini quiches, and berry tarts. My stomach growls, and I put my hand to it, ordering it to pipe down.

The door opens again and a servant intones, "Her Majesty, Queen Anna."

I stare, temporarily awestruck by the queen. She's so beautiful! Like a goddess of fertility with her long dark curly hair flowing over her bare shoulders in a navy blue sleeveless knit dress that hugs her rounded pregnant belly. She's carrying a large white leather purse.

"So good to meet you, Alice!" she exclaims.

I snap to attention, bow my head, and curtsy. "Your Majesty."

She stops in front of me, her brown eyes bright. "It's just the two of us today. Please call me Anna. Gabriel had some business to attend to, and I didn't want to delay our visit. Are you hungry? I'm starving."

"Yes." I follow her over to the seating area and take the

chair across from her. It's a firmly upholstered chair and it makes me sit a little straighter.

She pours the tea. So many things pop into my head—shouldn't a servant be doing that? Should I do that? We match in navy blue! How is your pregnancy going? Nothing comes out of my mouth. I'm tongue-tied.

"Sugar?" she asks.

"Yes, please." I'm thrilled that I can speak again and blurt, "Would you like me to serve you instead?"

She laughs as she uses silver tongs to drop a cube of light brown sugar into my tea. "I'm keeping it informal today. The servants and guards remain outside the parlor. We're both young American women, so I thought we could just hang like I used to with my friends back home." She gestures to the food. "Help yourself."

So I do, taking a tiny sandwich with cucumbers and a shiny blueberry tart, all while marveling that the queen of Villroy wants to hang with me. I take a sip of tea and scramble for something informal, American, and friendly to say. Baseball? Apple pie? Fourth of July?

She leans forward, her brown eyes sparkling. "I have to confess I'm a fangirl."

"Of what?"

"Of you! I read *The Duke's Dare* and *The Viscount's Victory*."

My lips form an O of surprise. The queen of Villroy read my stories? And then she shocks me even more by pulling the books out of her purse and handing me a pen. "Could you sign them?"

"Of course!" I take the pen and books from her and sign the inscription as though she's just a regular reader and not royal. The first for *The Duke's Dare* is a cheerful "Anna, dare to go further than is polite!" and the second, "Victory awaits the bold!" I sign my name with a flourish at the bottom.

She takes the books and pen back, smiling as she reads the inscriptions before tucking everything carefully into her purse. "Thanks! When do we get William's story? Are you writing it now?" That's the third book in the trilogy. He's a duke, a friend of the other two heroes.

"That was the plan." I go straight for the blueberry tart, in need of a sugar high, and take a huge bite.

"Was?"

I chew and swallow. "I'm finding it difficult to get back to writing happy love stories after the Ordeal."

She immediately catches on. "I give you a lot of credit for taking this trip solo. I'm sure you'll be writing again in no time. You just need some inspiration, right?"

I nod. "I actually came up with an idea yesterday, the first one I've had in months, but my editor hated it."

She crinkles her nose. "Sorry. What was it?"

"A love triangle where the men end up crushed. She said I was too bitter." I shrug one shoulder. "I guess I am."

Her eyes are sympathetic. "Anyone would need time to recover after expecting to be married and then not."

"Yes, well, I have to turn in three chapters by next week, a full draft in two weeks, and I've got nothing. I'm already past the extension I asked for so I could have time to plan my wedding." I sigh. "I'm basically looking at the end of my career, disappointing my loyal readers, and going home in utter defeat, tail between my legs."

She laughs, surprising me. "So dramatic. No wonder you're a writer."

"Anna, I'm not being dramatic. It's do-or-die time. Even worse, I'm completely unemployable. All I have is a bachelor's degree in history and no marketable skills."

"Girl, you're an award-winning, bestselling author! All you need is a seed of inspiration. Maybe Villroy or the palace will trigger something for you."

Her enthusiastic praise reassures me. Sometimes the voice in my head is too loud, shouting doomsday predictions that make it tough to move forward.

I find myself smiling. "Actually, Villroy has had a positive effect on me. Yesterday Lucas and I went out to the beach and—"

"Hold up. Lucas Rourke?"

"Um, yeah."

"How did you meet Lucas?" She takes a bite of ham sandwich, her eyes sparkling like I'm about to dish some good gossip.

I sip my tea, remembering the awful moment I met Lucas, and then the wonderful way I ended the day with him. "Yesterday I was in the courtyard speaking in a firm loud voice to my editor, trying to convince her my love-triangle idea could work, and he joined me, thinking I was in distress over a love triangle personally, which, ironically, I am. That was why my fiancé and I broke up. Love triangle with my best friend, which I guess I was subconsciously recreating in my awful story idea. Anyway, Lucas was very kind and just sat and listened to me. He's sensitive to women's feelings."

Her eyes bug out. "Lucas?" She gestures over her jaw. "The one with the beard?"

"Yes. Lucas Rourke."

"He's sensitive?"

"Very." I take a bite of cucumber sandwich, replaying all the ways he's been sensitive to my distress. He really has been wonderful and, without Riley to confide in, I haven't had much support. Oh, my parents were indignant on my behalf, but the truth is my social circle is small. Aside from some local writers I meet up with to talk shop, I used to spend most of my time with Riley and Mason. Now they have each other, and I'm alone. My nails dig into my palm, and I force myself to relax. That business is behind me now. The Ordeal was hell, and now I'm safely on the other side.

Anna takes a sip of tea, watching me over the rim. "So he talked to you and then what?"

I brighten, thinking of Lucas again. "He gave me his number so we could get together later and burn a picture of my ex, or whatever memento I might want to burn. You know, as sort of a goodbye thing to get him out of my head. I only had my honeymoon lingerie on hand, which, of course, reminded me of what I was supposed to use it for, so that seemed like a good candidate for burning." I lean forward. "You might be wondering why I brought the lingerie with me, and the answer is because it's beautiful and I thought I might like to wear it just for myself. Anyway, once we were on the beach last night with the soft sand and soothing waves under a starry moonlit sky, I had such a sense of contentment come over me that I didn't feel the need to burn anything after all. Having Lucas by my side made all the difference." I smile, remembering his oath to me. "He's a man of honor."

She blinks. "That was quite poetic. Was he, um…"

"What?"

"He's a charmer."

"Oh, he's much more than that! He's kind, sensitive, and understanding. In just one day he helped me turn things around, and I'm already feeling a lot better. Though maybe getting a good night's sleep helped too."

She smiles brightly. "I'm glad to hear it."

"He's very committed to Villroy's new business venture. I hope you know that about him too." I clamp my mouth shut on the rest of what Lucas told me about his frustrations with Anna and Gabriel regarding his place in the business. Damn, I fear I've said too much already.

"Forget I said that business part, please," I say. "Just know that he's a lot more than a globe-trotting, charming bachelor. He's deep and quite serious about his work."

Anna hides a smile behind her teacup.

"What?"

"You sound like you're into him."

I snort. "I swore off men."

She tilts her head with a smile. "That can change."

I busy myself arranging my cloth napkin over my lap, which I completely forgot to do in my nervous state over meeting the queen. "I don't kid myself that a gorgeous prince would ever be interested in me." *And I'm a hot mess.* I keep that to myself.

"What's wrong with you? You're smart, interesting, and accomplished."

"I'm far from men's ideal in terms of looks, and I'm a nerd on top of that." At her skeptical look, I whisper, "He dates movie stars."

She slices a hand through the air. "None of his movie stars have stuck. And so what if you're not movie-star beautiful? How many of us are? You have a lot going for you. I find you exquisite."

"Thanks," I manage over the lump in my throat. It's taken a lot to get to the confidence level I have today after bullying from girls in middle school, who called me a slut and spread vicious rumors about me just because I sprouted my large breasts early. I became a stress eater, which only made it worse in high school, where the popular beautiful girls called me fat and dumpy. Riley did what she could to help me deal, but it was tough to ignore all of it. I know my confidence level still needs work. I'll get there one day.

We eat in companionable silence for a few moments before she says, "I like Lucas. He's always been warm and fun, but, in the past, he's been flighty, taking off at a moment's notice, traveling around the world to meet up with friends and women. The globe-trotting party guy, you know? Gabriel's view of him is colored by the past, which makes him skeptical about handing over the reins for the business. Now after hearing your view of him, it's made me realize I need to come to my own conclusions about him and the man he is today. I want to give him a chance." She taps a scarlet red fingernail with rhinestones (or are they real diamonds?) against her red lips. "Maybe Lucas should take the lead with the bank meeting."

"I'm sure he'll do well with whatever you entrust him with."

She gives me a sly smile. "He's made quite an impression on you after just one day."

My cheeks flush, and I pop the rest of the blueberry tart in my mouth so I won't need to reply.

She leans forward and whispers, "I just had a crazy idea."

I quickly chew and swallow before leaning in. "What?"

"Before you say no, just think about it."

I slowly straighten, everything in me on full alert. "Your crazy idea involves me?"

"Yeah. You need a story, right?"

"Yes," I say slowly.

"And Lucas needs to look legit committed to our cause."

I'm on the edge of my seat. "And?"

She throws her hands up. "A fake engagement! It's perfect romance material. You pretend to be his fiancée, go to his meetings with him, and it will make him look like he's settling down. Everyone knows his rep as a globe-trotting hard-partying bachelor. You'll make him look the way he wants people to see him—respectable, solid, and committed. Honestly, I'd like to see him that way too."

My breath quickens. "Please don't say committed." Me and commitment are no longer friends.

"Okay, it makes him look *grounded*. Like someone you can depend on to see things through. It's like the perfect kill-two-birds-with-one-engagement idea."

"Am I the bird?"

She laughs. "No, silly, you're the author living the story. Then all you have to do is write it down. I'm brilliant! I just wrote your next book for you! Make sure you put me in the acknowledgments. Ooh! Maybe you could dedicate it to me. I've never had a book dedicated to me." She frames a caption in the air. "'A fake engagement to a royal romance.' You're welcome." She helps herself to a mini quiche and chews with a smug satisfied look on her face.

I'm utterly speechless for a full minute. Finally, I say, "But it's a lie."

She waves that away. "It's a creative invention for a good cause. No one will be the worse for wear, and engagements get called off all the time." Her brows lift, her brown eyes sparkling. "You could go with Lucas to royal events, too, not just stuffy banker meetings. Like a ball or a formal charity fundraiser dinner. Then all of it goes into your story, only you make it sound like Regency times. It's perfect!"

A creative invention. I do those all the time as a writer. Suddenly I can see it all clearly. Me as the heroine, Lucas as the duke avoiding the tedious attentions of every young miss of the ton who's dying to ensnare him. I could be his ward's governess, and then, with the help of his widowed aunt, I'm transformed into the belle of the ton. I'm his fake fiancée, which gives him some breathing room, and he will act besotted by me, err, her. They go through the motions for society—the balls, the formal teas, the drawing room courtship. All of it in name only because the heroine has her own reasons—she desperately wants to hang onto her family home in the country. The duke will settle the money on her that she needs to keep it in return for their charade. It's all there. Beginning and middle, and I just have to figure out the end. Maybe she'll end up with the duke, or maybe they'll both find a different love, better off for their brief connection and what they've taught each other.

I meet Anna's eyes, an understanding passing between us. This could work.

Just then the door bursts open and the man himself steps inside. I squeak, nearly rising to my feet, my cheeks hot.

"Did I miss anything?" Lucas asks, striding over to us.

"Hey, Lucas!" Anna calls cheerfully. "We were just talking about you. Have a seat."

7

Lucas

I take a seat between the two women and look around. "Where's Gabriel?"

Anna smiles, a secret knowing in her eyes. What is that about? "He couldn't make it."

Alice is very occupied with a cherry tart, slicing it in neat quarters. Her cheeks and neck are bright pink. What did she say about me? I told her more than I should have last night about my frustrations with Gabriel and Anna, which is why I'm here now. Damage control.

Anna serves me a cup of tea, still wearing a secret knowing look.

I can't stand the suspense. "What were you saying about me?"

"Alice had *a lot* to say," Anna says.

Alice's head jerks up. There's a bit of cherry filling on the corner of her lip, and her pink tongue darts out to lick it. I cannot look away. "I wasn't saying *a lot*," she protests.

"Yes, you were," Anna says cheerfully. "Don't be shy. Tell Lucas your brilliant idea."

Alice's jaw goes slack. Anna sends her a pointed look and inclines her head toward me.

"What brilliant idea?" I ask when no one seems likely to fill me in. "Alice?"

Her hand goes to her throat. "I-I mentioned that you've been very kind to me." She drops her hand and picks up her teacup, toasting me with it. "And I'm feeling a little better already." She takes a sip of tea.

"Oh." I relax and lean back in my seat, stretching my legs out.

"That's not all," Anna drawls like she's quite enjoying herself.

I narrow my eyes at her. "Whatever you're so excited about, just say it."

She takes a sip of tea, her eyes sparkling merrily. "Alice had the brilliant idea of a fake engagement to you."

Alice shakes her head vigorously. It must be another one of Anna's outrageous ideas. Her last one—the royal bachelor auction—was a blast.

I turn to Anna. "What in the world are you talking about?"

Anna beams. "It's perfect. For her, it'll give her the inspiration for the story she hasn't been able to write—fake engagements are all the rage—and for you, it would add an air of respect and legitimacy when you go to your meeting with the bankers."

My mind latches on to the last part. Meeting with the bankers? She's entrusting me with the raising of capital. "As CEO?" I want the authority and power behind the title, but also to have my name seen as the one leading Villroy forward. I have ideas for further expansion.

"I'll make you CFO for now. I'll work on getting you the other title for the future. I think after the baby arrives, Gabriel's priorities may shift, and he'll be more amenable to delegating." She rubs a hand over her stomach, smiling down at it.

I'm torn. Of course I want this opportunity, but why do I need a fiancée? Obviously Anna doesn't think I can pull it off on my own. I glance at Alice. Her blue eyes are wide and hopeful, her lower lip caught between her teeth. Hell. She needs this fake engagement for her story, and I can't bring myself to disappoint her after all she's been through.

I offer Anna my hand. "Deal."

She gives me a firm handshake back, looking immensely pleased.

I'm less pleased, but I tell myself the ends justify the means. I do want to be seen as the kind of man who is more than his rep. I want to be a man of substance. Society dictates marriage connotes respectability. I didn't make the rules; I merely play the game.

And it's not like I'm agreeing to a real relationship. I swore to Alice that I'm a man of honor, which means I won't be crossing the line with her, no matter how tempted I am. Besides, it's clear she's still hung up on her ex. And she's the worst kind of person for a relationship with me—tender-hearted, vulnerable, overly romantic. My hard realism would not go over well, and I do my best to avoid drama and messy entanglements. Still, we can be friends.

I offer Alice a small smile, and she gives me a shy smile in return. My chest puffs out with pride. Making her smile feels like a triumph every time, knowing the state she was in when she arrived. I can feel Anna's eyes on me, but I cannot look away from Alice's sweet smile.

"Ready to play the fiancée game with me?" I ask.

"Yes," she says softly.

"Good."

She takes a deep breath, her breasts rising noticeably in her snug dress.

I focus on drinking my tea, averting my gaze.

"Will there be balls?" she asks.

I nearly spew my tea. I did not expect that. Raunchy talk from sweet Alice? Is she propositioning me? "Fine by me," I manage.

"Great!" she exclaims. "That would really help my story."

Her stories must be sexier than I realized. Maybe I don't have to fight the attraction after all. This could be *fun*.

I give her my crooked, sexy smile.

"She means a formal ball, Prince Charming," Anna cuts in.

I shoot her a sour look, hiding my disappointment. "I knew that." I turn to Alice, and she's blushing.

She leans close and whispers, "Did you think I meant something dirty?"

"My mind works a well-worn dirty path," I say and smoothly shift away from temptation. "No formal ball. Likely a dinner. Is that a deal breaker?"

"Could there be a ball?" she presses. "I'd really like there to be a royal ball."

And suddenly I want to make that happen for her. She's helping me by stepping in as my fiancée for business purposes, and I want to do my part to help with her story. "I could look into it. There may be a ball in another kingdom."

"Excellent," Alice says, sounding enormously pleased. "Since this is for my story, which necessarily needs to be romantic, would you act the part and pull out all the princely stops?"

Anna kicks me under the table, and I slide her a dark look before turning back to Alice. "What princely stops do you mean? Like, flowers?"

She shakes her head. "You know, like, hand kissing." She demonstrates by lifting the back of her hand and placing a kiss on it, her eyes intent on mine. My nerve endings stir into awareness at the sensual pucker of her lips. She drops her hand. "As well as courtly bows and draping your cape across a puddle for me to walk over. Stuff like that."

Is she serious? She sounds serious.

"Err…cape? I don't wear a cape." Am I supposed to dress like a relic from Regency England? I'm afraid to ask.

She huffs. "If I have to teach you how to be a proper romantic prince, it won't work at all." She shakes her head. "Something is seriously lacking in your princely education."

I bite back a smile. "Maybe you should take that up with my mother, the former queen."

"Oh! I would never..." She blushes and glances at Anna, who looks like she's watching a fascinating documentary called How Lucas Sucks at Being a Regency-Era Fiancé. In my defense, any man would.

I gesture toward the door. "Let's see her right now."

Alice leans so close I catch her flowery scent. "*Lucas.* Please. You're embarrassing me in front of the queen."

Anna holds out a book to me. The cover has a man in a black suit with his arm around a woman in a red dress. It says *The Duke's Dare* in flowing script. It's Alice's book. "Read this," she says. "It'll tell you everything you need to know about pulling out all the stops. And don't bend the pages or crack the cover. This is my prized signed copy."

The book looks way too romantic and girly. I can feel Alice's eyes boring into me. Then I remember she told me her idiot ex criticized her book and never even read it. And she's an award-winning, bestselling author. It says so right on the cover. Surely a man of honor can do better than her ex and read the damn thing. Just as long as my brothers don't catch me with it.

I take the book. "Thank you. I'm sure it will be an interesting read."

Alice gives me a sweet smile, and my heart thumps a little harder.

Anna nudges my shoulder. "By the way, your mom is on her way to the US, so you're off the hook with the whole lacking-princely-education deal." She smiles. "Your mom's going to visit Silvia, and then she's going to check out a spa for cancer patients and people recovering from it to see about adding the recovery massage service to our spa. It's the kind of thing your dad and mine could've benefited from." Both of us lost our fathers to cancer.

I take a sip of tea, easing the tightness in my throat. "That would be a great add-on."

Anna is quiet for a moment, her eyes shiny. Her loss was more recent. Mike was her foster dad, and she looked after him devotedly. She sips her tea and puts her cup down. "It's an honor to them both."

"Agreed," I say.

She turns to Alice, changing the subject. "So, any ideas sparking for your story?"

Alice looks to the ceiling for a long moment before saying, "We've already met the hero with inky black hair and glittering blue eyes. And the heroine will have long golden tresses, lively green eyes, and a fair complexion with a hint of pale pink. Diana is his ward's governess."

Anna leans over and whispers to me, "She sounds British."

"Shh, don't interrupt," I return. "She said she's been stuck for a while."

Anna speaks anyway, doing her own thing as usual. "Alice, don't you think Lucas's aquamarine eyes are stunning?"

Both women stare at me, and I try not to blink. And, yes, my eyes are stunning. Women comment on them all the time. I wait impatiently for Alice to agree, but she remains quietly staring.

Anna goes on, staring into my eyes. "We know William's eyes are blue, but couldn't they be aquamarine blue up close? I've always marveled at Gabriel's eyes. It's a family trait. They match the sea here."

Alice slowly turns from my eyes and tells Anna, "They're certainly striking, but I'm not writing a memoir. It needs to be an Alice Segal original based on my previous world and loosely drawn from our fake-engagement premise."

Anna mouths, "British," at me before saying out loud, "Okay, then. Better get started."

Alice abruptly stands. "You're right. Thank you for everything, Anna. I will totally dedicate this book to you."

Anna grins. "Excellent."

"What am I, chopped liver?" I ask in a mock aggrieved tone. "The fiancé doesn't get a nod?"

Alice is already halfway to the door, muttering to herself.

I take my leave of Anna, giving her a small bow before catching up with Alice.

"When do you need to turn in this Alice Segal original?" Anna calls just as we reach the door.

Alice halts, her shoulders drooping. She turns. "First draft in two weeks. The final manuscript in six weeks."

Anna waves her hand in the air like she's granting a wish. "Then I hereby grant you the use of the guest suite for the next six weeks free of charge."

My gaze collides with Alice's. The air is suddenly sucked out of the room as the first lick of panic hits me. I tear my gaze away. *Six weeks.*

That's long enough to form an attachment.

I mean, not for me. I'll be fine. I never get attached. Not since…it's Alice I'm concerned about. She just went through a brutal breakup. I can already see the drama that would follow if she became attached to me, and I do *not* want to go there. I need to be crystal clear that we're playing a game. It's the only way to keep things light.

"Thank you!" Alice exclaims to Anna, and then takes off, muttering, "Good thing I never got a cat."

Cat? Maybe she means there's no one to feed her imaginary cat back home if she stays here for six weeks. Her mind works in unusual, fascinating ways.

I slowly turn back to Anna, suspicious for the first time. Was this not a straightforward gesture to test my abilities in the business, but instead a matchmaking setup?

She gives me a sly smile. "Better hurry up and get an engagement ring."

I open my mouth and then close it again. Best not to look a gift horse in the mouth or, in this case, an unconventional queen with mysterious ways of getting things done. I'm CFO. It's a step in the right direction and that's all that matters.

～

Alice

My mind is a whirl of governess and duke, Diana and William, in their early encounters. Her—deferential with a beauty hidden to most under her drab clothing and cap. Him —dashing, only occasionally aware of his governess as she cares for his ward, a seven-year-old girl some whisper is his bastard daughter, but is actually his deceased cousin's child. He cares not what society thinks, but he's nearing the age where he must secure an heir. And he's finding the marriage mart of the London Season insufferable.

I halt at an unexpected dead end in the palace, where I thought the stairs would be. Crap. I thought it was left, long hallway, right, right to the stairs. Where am I? They should have signs around here. Of course, now that I'm desperate to get to my laptop to write all this down, I can't find a servant anywhere to help. I could dictate into my phone, but I know more will come out with my fingers on the keyboard if I can just get to my laptop and let it flow. I might even have the first chapter.

I pull out my phone and text Lucas. *I'm lost and I need to get back to my room STAT.*

A text pings back a moment later. *Where are you?*

I don't know! If I knew, I wouldn't be lost. I went left and then right, right.

I look around and text again. *There's a Viking warrior shield on the wall. I'm in a dead end. Still on the first floor.*

Don't move.

I pull out the notes app on my phone and type a couple of sentences as quickly as I can for chapter one.

"Found you!" Lucas calls. "You're in the west wing, and you want to be in the east wing."

"Okay, let's go."

He offers me his arm in a gallant gesture that momentarily stalls my brain. I stare at it, his gray shirt stretching across a nicely rounded bicep, close enough to touch. He wants me to touch. His aquamarine eyes meet mine—they *are* stunning—a ghost of a smile crossing his lips. "You did want me to pull out all the princely stops, right? As your duke inspiration." He's playing the Regency fake-engagement game for me!

My lashes lower, warmth stealing through me. "Yes, thank you." I place my hand on his forearm, instantly feeling his warmth through the soft fabric of his shirt as he leads us out of the dead end. My mouth goes dry, my mind absolute mush. I am living my story, and it's surreal. It's a game. Can't forget that.

He walks with a confident, regal air, seeming even more princely fiancé. "My pleasure, Miss Segal." Even his voice is drier and more proper, reminiscent of the duke in my mind.

"Thank you, Your Grace." And then I'm so excited, I break character. "This has already gotten my brain cranking! I've got the beginning and middle." *Though I'm rapidly losing it, given your proximity*, I add silently.

"That's good news, Miss Segal."

"Please call me Alice."

"Only if you address me by my given name."

"Yes, of course, Lucas," I whisper and then get quiet. I'm extremely conscious of just how close he is, how warm his arm feels, how good he smells, like spice and soap. This is how the duke will smell in my story.

"So, Alice, how will it end?"

"Happily," I say absently. "My stories always end happily." But exactly how? I don't know.

"I meant our engagement. Not the fictional one."

"I don't know. What do you think?"

"We found we weren't compatible."

"There needs to be a better reason than that." I think on this. "I'd really prefer if it wasn't another woman. My readers already know I called off my wedding because my fiancé cheated."

His brows shoot up. "You told your readers?"

"I shared the wedding details for months on social media. It was romantic and on brand for me. I had to explain why it was called off."

"Won't it look bad that you're engaged again so soon?"

"I'm not going to tell anyone. I told my readers I was taking a break from social media to heal. But you're right, realistically, with you being who you are—Prince Lucas Rourke, world's most eligible royal bachelor—eventually the news will get out, so we should know how the engagement ends to manage the message."

He looks thoughtful. "Maybe you get a job offer overseas, and I don't want to uproot since my place is here. That happened to me in real life before, just another example of how I'm rooted in Villroy."

"That totally works, except I would switch it up, make it like adventure calls. A new business venture in America that's quite lucrative. After the war of eighteen twelve in America, there was a huge push for American manufacturing and construction of a transportation system."

"Ah, Miss Segal, it seems we're back in Regency times."

"I really need to get to my laptop." I pull away and slip off my heels, preparing to run. "I see the stairs up ahead, and then it's just two left turns, right?"

"Are you ditching your new fiancé so soon?" he asks in a teasing voice.

"I need to write. Thank you for your help. I'm going to make a run for it."

"No."

"No?"

He gives me his crooked sexy smile. "Surely you know women don't run *from* me. They run *to* me. I'm irresistibly charming."

I hesitate. There's something about his charming snark that works for me.

He goes on. "So back to our previous topic, the engagement ends when you need to return to the US for work reasons. Maybe your next book is set partially in America, and you need to immerse yourself in research."

"Book," I echo, adrenaline racing through me. I need to get to work. "Perfect. Gotta run!"

I take a step and come up short, face to chest with him. He's blocking me! "Lucas!"

His eyes dance with good humor. "Alice!"

I run around him, and we race through the palace. I can barely catch my breath, exhilarated.

"Here you are," he says, slightly out of breath when we finally reach my room. "Technically, we ran together, so my stellar rep with women still stands—no woman has ever run from me."

I put a hand to my heaving bosom, majorly out of breath. "You'll do a lot for that rep of yours." I pause, catching my breath. "Woo! That got the blood flowing, and my brain cranking once more."

He takes my hand and lifts it toward his lips, his aquamarine eyes smoldering into mine. My heart thunders in my chest. This is so going in my book! But then he doesn't kiss it, instead he holds our hands up, palm to palm, studying our fingers, and then strokes down the length of my ring finger in a gesture that's strangely erotic.

"What was that?" I breathe.

"I'm estimating your ring size to find you a suitable engagement ring." His voice is silky smooth. "Must keep up appearances."

I pat over my heart. "Well, pitter-pat, those were some princely moves you just did for me. Thanks for that inspiration. Let me make it easy for you. I'm a size six ring, and I know this because I recently had my ring sized down after I lost weight for my wedding gown and…" I trail off. It was Mason's idea that I lose weight so I'd look good in the wedding pictures. He broached the subject the day after he proposed. The implication that I didn't currently look good had me in a shame cycle of crash dieting and chocolate eating that I'm just now breaking away from. This sobers me. I changed myself so much to please Mason I almost didn't know who I was anymore. No wonder I couldn't write. It wasn't just being busy with wedding preparations. I lost myself.

"Alice?"

I exhale sharply. "You don't have to buy me a ring."

"Of course I do. Every fiancée needs a ring."

I shake my head, and he nods his. He's a man used to getting his way, a charming, gorgeous prince with women falling at his feet. Even knowing this, I cave. "Well, don't spend a lot. I mean, what if your real fiancée doesn't wear a size six ring?"

"Let me worry about that. Would you like a Regency-era ring?"

My heart squeezes. "That's so thoughtful of you. Actually, it wasn't common to wear an engagement ring back then, though sometimes the man would wear a promise ring woven of his beloved's hair."

He grimaces. "I'll pass on the hair ring."

I lift a lock of my hair and wave it at him. "Are you sure? It's nice and soft."

"Is it?"

A tense beat passes, his eyes locked on mine.

My breathing accelerates. "Yes." Does he want to play with my hair? I love that.

He looks away, muttering, "I'll have to take your word for it." He shoves his hands in his pockets and takes a step back. "Good luck with your writing."

"Thanks."

I watch as he turns and strides away, his posture stiff. It's strange how he suddenly became so tense after the easy way we've been together. This is not good. We have to look comfortable with each other to be a believable couple.

"Wait!" I hurry to catch up with him.

He turns and grins. "I told you women run to me."

I laugh, glad he's back to his laid-back charming self. "Seems like it got a little weird back there when I offered to let you touch my hair, which is totally *not* a requirement of a fake fiancé, but people will expect a certain comfortable intimacy between us."

He stiffens, his gaze darting to the side. "What do you mean exactly?"

I don't know where this is coming from, but somehow it makes perfect sense. We need to move past any awkwardness to be believable. "We should practice kissing so it looks natural, don't you think?"

He clears his throat. "I…well, it seems…" His gaze shifts all around me, not quite meeting my eyes.

I stifle a sigh. This is not going how I hoped. He's not tempted by me in the least.

I step kissing close, deciding we just need to go for it. "You do want to be believable, don't you? Just kiss me."

"On the lips?"

I huff. "Where else would you kiss me? Wait. Never mind. You know what I mean. What's the problem? You don't want to kiss your fiancée?"

He swallows visibly. "No, I mean yes, of course we should practice."

I close my eyes and wait impatiently.

Nothing.

I crack an eye open. He's somehow stiffened even more, his arms straight at his sides, his gaze just past my ear. "Lucas!" I hiss.

He leans down and gives me a peck on the lips. And before I can shift us into real kiss territory, he puts his hands on my shoulders, turns me, and gives me a little shove back toward my room. "Go write."

I rush back to my room, cheeks burning, equal parts disappointed and embarrassed. I'll have to lean on my imagination to fill in the good parts.

8

I'm in my study the next afternoon going over the business finances in preparation for the meeting with the bankers when there's a knock at the door. "Come in."

Gabriel strides in and stops in front of my desk. "A fake engagement. Bold but misguided."

I close the laptop and suppress a sigh.

It occurs to me that Anna could've conveniently not claimed responsibility for the idea. She's probably sticking with her story that it was Alice's idea, and Gabriel probably thinks I went along with it because I let my cock lead the way, as usual. But I'm not going to point a finger at Anna. I won't do anything to cause a rift between her and Gabriel.

I spear a hand through my hair. "Look, it's not a big deal. I went over all the angles and there's literally no downside."

He shakes his head. "I understand you want to spend time with Alice, but this is not the way. It's too far. The lie will come out and then no one will trust us." He blows out a breath. "We finally set things right after Emma ran away from her own wedding and her wretched ex told anyone who would listen that our family was rife with dishonorable, cheating liars. You'll only rekindle those flames. And word will spread. Our family's reputation will be ruined beyond repair. No bank will take a meeting with us once the deception is revealed." Emma is our younger sister, and she was right to bail on her wedding.

"It won't be revealed. You're overreacting. This is nothing like what happened with Emma. It's a harmless white lie."

He clenches his jaw. "You're right that this isn't like when Emma ran scared. It's worse. It's deliberately misleading people. I'm asking you to stop. Spend time with Alice in some other way."

How can I let Alice down by cancelling our engagement plan when she's so ecstatic about the inspiration? Just to appease my brother's unfounded worries? No, I refuse.

"It can only help with the bankers," I say. "I'll look less like a party guy, more serious and committed, which I am, by the way, *completely* committed to this business. I just need to present a new image."

"Lucas, if you go through with this, the only recourse we'd have in the event of the inevitable public relations nightmare is to disassociate ourselves from you and your dishonesty. You could never have anything to do with our business again. Neither of us wants that."

I silently seethe, furious at the threat of cutting me off permanently, but not trusting myself to speak.

He turns and strides to the door, stopping with his hand on the knob. "I understand her appeal. Anna is quite taken with her. Just keep business and pleasure separate. I'm sure you'll present to the bankers just fine on your own with all your experience as an angel investor."

"Thank you." I appreciate the vote of confidence even if I don't agree with dropping the fake engagement. Improving my image by looking like a committed man can only help.

He lets himself out.

I stare at the desk. Am I willing to risk my place in the business to stick to the fake engagement? Yes. I want this bank loan to go through with me as CFO as quickly as possible. Then I'll have proven myself for my ultimate goal of becoming CEO. Even Gabriel still sees me as the globe-trotting party guy. It's why he won't give me any real authority. The ends justify the means. And I can't let Alice down.

What Gabriel doesn't know won't hurt him.

~

I had dinner with Alice last night at her request, though I was reluctant at first. My attraction to her grows every time I see her, and I don't want to get too close. I admit I agreed to dinner out of a sense of obligation, so we could fill each other in on the stuff an engaged couple should know about each other. She dashed off immediately afterward to write more of her long-overdue story. Bit of an ego hit that she prefers her laptop to prolonging our time together, but it's probably for the best.

Her natural good humor made it easy to say yes to tonight's dinner. The conversation is relaxed and, as long as there's some distance between us, our time together is all in good fun. I watch as she digs into her chocolate mousse, her expression rapturous. She loves chocolate more than anything. I can take it or leave it.

Tomorrow night, Friday, we'll meet Gabriel's friend, the banker Jules Marchand, and his wife, Celeste, for dinner in Paris. Gabriel knows them from the charity-dinner circuit. I told Jules in our brief phone call that I'd be bringing my famous author fiancée, and it turns out his wife is a big fan. This fake engagement is working out even better than I thought, and I'm glad I stuck with it. Alice will be a boon to me at the dinner, so, in return, I've arranged for us to spend the weekend for some sightseeing. She's never been to Paris.

I didn't tell Anna I was still planning on bringing Alice to the meeting, not wanting to sow discord between her and Gabriel. I also didn't tell Alice that Gabriel told me not to play fake fiancé with her. It's just one meeting. By the time anyone notices that Alice and I are away together, the deal will be done.

I take a sip of brandy, contemplating what goes on in Alice's creative brain. I read her book *The Duke's Dare* the same night I got it in an attempt to distract myself from thinking about our practice kiss. I held back with that kiss, trying to keep my distance, but I didn't miss how soft her lips were, her sexy scent, the pink of her cheeks. In any case, the story was smart, witty, emotional, and extremely sexy. Her duke might have formal manners, but he certainly was no slouch in the bedroom. Though he did spout some flowery words no man would ever spout in the heat of passion. I can only conclude that Alice has never truly felt the heat of passion. What can you expect when she dates men like her geeky ex?

Not my business.

But, hell, sometimes it is. Her ex keeps leaving her voice-mails and sending texts pleading with her to talk. She says he probably wants to apologize. Like that can make up for what he did. *Break up and move on!* A good reminder that I don't need the complication of getting embroiled in her drama. I've got enough trouble of my own trying to take my rightful place in the business.

A short while later, I escort Alice back to her room, keeping her hand tucked in the crook of my elbow, which I've learned is the only way to prevent her from sprinting to her laptop. Last night when she made a run for it, she nearly knocked over our oldest servant. Albert held onto her arms for balance and then pretended it was him helping her, intoning, "Steady there, ma'am."

My mind skips ahead to tomorrow night's dinner meeting. I should go over the numbers again tonight to be sure I have them memorized.

Alice turns to me. "Are you super nervous about tomorrow night, or just a little nervous?" Funny how she can sense that. She's remarkably in tune with me. Most people just see my casual easygoing smile and believe there's nothing deeper.

"Which part would I be nervous about? Convincing the

banker, playing engaged to a woman I just met three days ago, or proving myself to Gabriel?"

She gives me a gentle smile. "Aww, you're super nervous." She stops walking and looks up at me, gazing deep into my eyes. I get the sudden feeling that she can see the real me without all the charming princely trappings. "Listen, you and I are perfectly believable as a couple. We know all the important stuff, and I've got the ring." She holds up her hand, showing off the round ruby surrounded by a ring of diamonds. It's from the royal vault. She's unaware of the value, or that it was my grandmother's ring. I told her I had it express delivered from an online jeweler and that the ruby was imperfect, so it was a bargain. It was the only way I could get her to wear it.

She gets distracted by the ring, turning it this way and that. "You must need a microscope to see the imperfection in this ruby. It looks perfect to me. I can't believe you got this at a bargain. What a steal!"

I murmur noncommittally.

She meets my eyes again, seeming to remember herself, and says fiercely, "You are a badass businessman. You've got this. You did your due diligence and this will go great. So just imagine us celebrating afterward with champagne, okay?" She smiles, and my heart thumps harder. Her smile does that to me. It used to feel like a triumph to see it emerge; now it feels like a gift.

I gaze into her bright blue eyes, momentarily dazed. It's not just her smile. It's that she sees past the hard-partying rep I've cultivated. She *believes* in me. That means something, especially now while I'm working so hard to prove myself in the family business.

I tear my gaze away. "Thanks for the vote of confidence." I resume our walk to her suite, tucking her hand in the crook of my arm. "It's far from a sure thing, and Gabriel is a whole other matter. I don't know what it will take to make him see what I'm capable of."

"Maybe he's a gotta-see-it-to-believe-it kind of guy. So

you'll show him. You got this, tiger!" She pulls her hand from my elbow and gives me a soft punch to the bicep. Somewhere along the way she got comfortable with me. Royals are untouchable for the most part.

"Fair warning," she says, "I'm not much for small talk. I'm just going to follow your lead and smile in the background as your fiancée."

"Now you tell me," I tease. "I'm going to have to do all the hard work."

She snaps her fingers at me. "Quick, what's my favorite food?"

"Anything chocolate. What are my siblings' names?"

"Ooh, I know this one! Age order: Gabriel, Phillip, then you, Oscar, Emma, Adrian, and Silvia. Adrian and Silvia are twins. The younger sons are more laid-back than the heir and the spare because you were raised with different expectations—"

"And because we're naturally wonderful."

"Yes, of course," she says breezily, and it occurs to me that maybe she does think I'm wonderful. She hasn't met Oscar and Adrian yet. Something in me shifts, a warmth radiating through my chest as she rattles off random facts about my family. "Emma married Jackson Walker." She pauses. "You have a lot of glamorous people in your family."

"Just Jackson. He's a rock legend. Too bad you missed him. He and Emma left the day before you arrived for their honeymoon."

"Bummer. But it's not just him that's glam. It's all of you. You know, the royal thing."

"I suppose it could be seen that way, though when you're living it…maybe less so."

She shakes her head. "Whatever you say."

I don't share further about the downside—the lack of privacy, the constant shadow of the guards, the overzealous paparazzi. It's not a bad life. It's just not glamorous all the time.

"Let's see, what else?" she asks, continuing before I can

reply, "Phillip is the spare and the UN Ambassador for Clean Water." She looks thoughtful, her brows knit together, her lips pursed. "The twins must miss each other. Adrian wasn't at Yale with Silvia, and now he lives here and she's in the US. Twins have a special bond, don't they?"

Her mind twists and turns all over the place. It's never a dull moment talking to her. "They were close as kids. They're grown now. Back to us, how did we meet?"

She lifts a finger in the air. "Mutual friends. I was invited to dinner at my agent's country house in Connecticut, and you were there because you went to university with her husband."

"Frank Wexler," I return, supplying the name of my supposed friend. "Which university did we attend?"

"Oxford because you're a smartie, and you didn't get any special treatment just because you're a royal."

I grin. "You can leave that last part out. I don't want to sound like I'm bragging." I only told her that because I didn't want her to think I skated through Oxford. She's incredibly bright and values education.

She bumps her shoulder into my arm. "I can brag about you. I'm your fiancée. You studied PPE, which is philosophy, politics, and economics all in one major."

"And you studied history at Yale and wrote your first book while you were still a student there as a way to relax."

She beams. "Correct. Where am I from?"

"Portland, Oregon."

"That's where I live now. I grew up in—"

"Gresham, Oregon."

"Very good!"

"We've been together for three months. That's all it took."

Her blue eyes sparkle behind her glasses. "You fell *hard*. Like a total face-plant at my feet. On our first date you told me you were going to marry me."

I rock my head side to side, biting my tongue. We had a bit of back-and-forth on that point, but I ultimately let her have it because she found the idea so romantic. "Okay, but we don't need to harp on that, yeah? Let's just say we fell for each other."

"And then you spent the next month convincing me to marry you with numerous romantic gestures because you were so hopelessly besotted." She loves that word, *besotted*. It sounds to me like a sappy idiot, but to her it's dreamy with love. "Once you flew all the way to Portland for my birthday just to make me my favorite double fudge cake, even though you had to fly back the very next day for an important meeting with the contractors that you have personally super-vised on a daily basis at the Island Bliss Spa."

I smile. She's good, weaving in my dedication to her and the project. "Your birthday is May first. And you were also besotted; otherwise you wouldn't have accepted my proposal."

"Yes," she says dreamily. "Your birthday is June first. Twenty-nine and holding up nicely. Isn't it cute how we were both born on the first? There must be some astrological signif-icance there. Astrology was very popular during the Regency—"

I cut her off because Regency history can take a very long time. "Sounds like fate. And the wedding is…?"

"The wedding isn't until next June because a royal wedding requires a lot of planning."

I smile. "Yes. I think we've got this couple thing down."

Her phone rings, and she flushes guiltily. I've told her numerous times just to block him. "I'd better check in case it's my parents." She pulls her phone from her small purse and smiles. "It's my editor. She's probably just checking in about the three chapters I owe her. I'm almost there." She punches the button, gives a cheery hello, and then gets quiet, listening.

I'm thinking of heading to my study to go over the numbers again when she grabs my arm in a tight grip, stilling me. Her voice is strained. "Yes, I understand. I will. Thank you, Quinn. I promise I'll have it to you." She pauses. "Okay, bye."

"What's wrong?"

She puts her phone away and blows out a breath. "My publisher in New York wants me to come in for a meeting. Quinn says they want to cancel the contract because of the delays. She's asked me to send six chapters by tomorrow, and she'll try to hold them off as long as she can. I've nearly got three, which I hoped to finish tomorrow." She bites her lower lip. "I'm sorry, Lucas. I don't know if I can make it to your dinner in Paris tomorrow night."

I stare at her in alarm. "What do you mean? That was the whole point of this fake engagement. I already told Jules I was bringing you. Celeste can't wait to meet you. She's a fan of your work."

She grimaces. "I'm going to lose my job if I don't get something decent in my editor's hands tomorrow. I need the time."

My gut churns. I didn't realize just how much I needed her at the dinner until this moment. Not just for being a famous author or improving my image, I needed her for being her, a source of support. "Just stay up late tonight and get it done."

"I'll try, but I know myself. Even on my best days, I can only write so fast."

I clench my jaw. "We had a deal." I hate that I need her.

"I'll really try, I promise. Maybe I can meet you there. You can go early and send the jet back for me. You said it's a short flight, right? And dinner isn't until eight."

"Fine," I grumble. "I'll meet you there at eight. Unless you get done before that."

She nods once and races into her suite.

I turn and stride away, telling myself to calm the fuck down, but it's impossible. This meeting is too important. I've built her into my plans, and she can't screw them up.

9

———

Lucas

The jet begins its descent, and my stomach drops with it. Damn nerves again. I'm well prepared for my dinner meeting. If it goes well, I'll likely be invited to a formal meeting at the bank next week. Only problem is, Alice isn't with me.

I checked in with her at noon in her suite, and she was in a state, frazzled and apologetic, before dashing back to her laptop and calling over her shoulder, "I swear I'll try to meet you!" She's on chapter four and not happy with it yet. I understand her urgency—her job is on the line—but I can't help but wish I never agreed to this fake engagement because now I'm entangled more than I want to be. I need her and, though I wish it was otherwise, I *want* her. More than is reasonable. It's horrible. I'm never this twisted up over a woman. Women get twisted up over me.

By the time I make it to the restaurant shortly before eight, I'm wound tight. I text her one last time. She turned her phone off to work, and I'm hoping she's finished her chapters, turned the phone back on, and on her way to me. No response. Dammit.

A few minutes later, a man in his thirties with dark brown hair parted to the side approaches me with a smile, greeting me in French, and then introducing himself and his wife, Celeste. I respond warmly in French.

They both exclaim over me. "I'd know you anywhere," Jules says. "Except for the beard, you look just like Gabriel."

I force a smile. "There's a strong family resemblance with all of my brothers."

"It's uncanny," Celeste murmurs. She looks around. "Is Alice here? I brought some books for her to sign." She shows me a tote bag filled with at least a dozen paperbacks. "When I told my friends I was having dinner with her tonight, they asked me to have their books signed too. Do you think she'll mind?"

"I'm sure she'd be happy to. She's going to be a little late due to a work thing."

Celeste smiles eagerly. "Is it her next story?"

"Yes."

"Should we wait for her?" Jules asks.

"I'll check in with her one more time." I text in irritated jabs, asking once again if she's on her way. No response. Did she forget to turn her phone back on, or is she still writing? She's driving me crazy!

I let out a breath. "I think it's going to be a while. Let's go in." I signal the maître d', and a few moments later we're escorted to a private room in the back of the restaurant, where a corner table is set for us. The other three tables in the space are empty. My two guards remain posted just outside the entrance of the room.

Dinner is a leisurely affair, the talk about everything but business; that will come at the end of the meal. I do my best to keep up my side of the conversation while still on alert, keeping an eye out for Alice.

Dinner's over two hours later, the dishes are cleared, and still no Alice. I don't even bother to text her, embarrassed that my fiancée has stood me up.

The cheese course arrives. No Alice.

Dessert course arrives. I even ordered a chocolate soufflé, hoping in some cosmic way it would attract her. What the hell is wrong with me? This is not who I am, so fixated on a woman.

Jules finally gets down to business. I force myself to focus on his questions. I can't screw this up with thoughts of Alice. After a lengthy conversation, he seems interested yet hasn't asked me for a more formal meeting to make it official. I'm trying to decide how much to push for next steps when Celeste lifts a hand, saying excitedly, "Hello, Alice! Over here!"

I nearly collapse with relief and stand to greet my extremely late fiancée.

~

Alice

I did it! Nothing like an impossible deadline to get the words flowing. My fingers were flying across the keyboard, typos all over the place, but it didn't matter because I got the feeling I missed for so long, the deep flow of creativity. The best part is, Quinn just texted that she loved the chapters I sent, and told me she's confident my contract will hold as long as I turn in the first draft by next week. I'm back, baby! She changed my title, though. I had called it *The Duke's Arrangement*, and she changed it to *The Scoundrel and the Governess*. Marketing loved her title, so that's what it is now. I suppose the duke is a scoundrel the way he's using his governess as a shield from the more eligible women of the ton. And he's already stolen kisses from her. I have a feeling he'll become more and more of a scoundrel as the story goes on.

I'm exhausted but happy, and it looks like I made it in time for dessert, my favorite meal. I leave my suitcase and laptop with the royal guard who greeted me, and take in Lucas striding toward me in a dark gray suit. He does not look happy. Uh-oh. I hope his meeting didn't go poorly.

"Hi!" I say brightly. "I made it. Sorry I'm late."

He leans down and kisses my cheek, playing the fiancé game. "I texted you."

"I saw it when I was on the jet. I texted you back, but you were probably busy with dinner." I lower my voice. "How's it going?"

He takes my hand and guides me back to the table without a word. Is he mad that I was late? I raced all day just so I could make it here.

We arrive at the table, and Lucas places a hand on my lower back, distracting me with the touch. He's touched me very little, and I'm terribly aware of the warmth and pressure of his hand through the thin fabric of my dress. "This is my fiancée, Alice. Alice, this is Jules and his lovely wife, Celeste."

"Hello, so nice to meet you both," I say.

They both give me warm hellos. Lucas pulls out my chair for me, a very princely gesture, before taking the seat next to me. I'm thoroughly enjoying playing engaged couple so far. It's like living the romance without all that messy real-world emotional angst. Between that and getting back into the writing groove, I'm feeling so much better.

Celeste smiles at me. "We were saying earlier how much Lucas resembles Gabriel. Except for the beard, it's like twins."

I nod. "Not quite twins. Lucas's forehead isn't as prominent, his nose is a touch narrower, and he's undoubtedly the more handsome of the two." So I did a little Rourke research online, marveling over the strong resemblance of the Rourke brothers, all five of them with thick dark brown hair, angular cheekbones, square jaw, full lips. The aquamarine eyes are a family trait as well, except for Adrian, who has hazel eyes.

Lucas smiles widely. "Spoken like a besotted fiancée, eh?"

He's not mad at me. I think.

I hitch a thumb toward him. "That's him too. He asked me to marry him on our very first date!"

Celeste and Jules laugh. I glance at Lucas, a small rueful smile playing over his lips. "I told her to keep that quiet," he says with a wink.

"Ah, young love," Celeste says. "Shall we order you something, Alice?"

"No, thanks. I ate earlier at the palace to power through my chapters."

Lucas slides his dessert over to me. "I ordered you chocolate soufflé. It's still warm."

"Thank you! What a great reward after today's work." I dig in to warm chocolate heaven.

Lucas turns to Jules and speaks French like a native, startling me. He does have a unique accent in English, more proper and formal than mine with a bit of a lilt. Now I realize it's a French lilt, and he must be bilingual. I quickly recover, returning my attention to my dessert. That's the kind of thing a fiancée would know. Celeste chimes in on the conversation too. I have no idea what they're saying. I fear I'm in for a long stretch of pasting on fake clueless smiles. I'll probably develop a tic. Or I could join the conversation, spouting my menu French—éclair, croissant, quiche. I'm sure that would impress everyone. Not.

After the dessert dishes are cleared, the waiter pours cognac in snifters for us. Jules and Lucas are still speaking in French. It sounds more serious now.

I take a sip of cognac. Wow, that is strong.

Celeste leans across the table toward me. "While the men talk business, I have to confess I'm a big fan of your work."

"Oh, thank you! That's so nice to hear." And in English too!

"Would you mind signing your book for me?"

"Of course! Let me see if I have a pen." I dig around in my purse. "They always seem to fall to the bottom. Aha!" Oh, I do know another French word. "Voila!" I amend, holding up a pen triumphantly, and then stare in shock. There's three stacks of the French translation of *The Duke's Dare* in front of Celeste.

"A few for my friends too if you don't mind," she says hopefully.

"Happy to," I say, reaching for the first stack. "It will be in

English, but I do know how to say happy reading. *Bonne lecture!*"

"Wonderful!" she exclaims and then spends the next several minutes telling me who to make the books out to. There's a ton of Maries in her friend circle.

After I finish, she thanks me profusely, tucking the books carefully back in her bag.

It's so nice to be appreciated after writing my ass off all night and day. "No problem at all! I'm always happy to meet a reader and happy to sign."

She leans forward. "You must be so busy writing your story and planning a wedding, no?"

I nearly blurt that the wedding got cancelled when I realize she means my wedding to Lucas. He catches my eye, and I stumble over the words I'm supposed to say. "Yes, um, it does take a lot of planning. The palace chapel has to be prepared and, you know, flowers, food, and the invitations. You're invited, of course, and, well, it'll be a while."

She smiles. "I look forward to it."

Lucas keeps up his business conversation in French, so I guess I didn't screw up the delayed wedding explanation. I ask Celeste about herself, and it turns out she's a lawyer.

"A banker and a lawyer. Sounds like a very serious household," I blurt.

She laughs. "Our sons keep it from ever being too serious." She pulls her phone out of her purse and shows me a pair of dark-haired little boys with mischievous matching smiles.

"They must keep you running."

She smiles at their picture and then puts the phone away. "They certainly do."

We chat a little more and then we all say our goodbyes. I'm not sure if it went well for Lucas because his expression gives nothing away. I excuse myself to the ladies' room, telling Lucas I'll meet him in the lobby.

When I return, it's just Lucas and his two beefy guards. They're new to me, and I don't know their names. I'm secretly calling them Hercules (the thick-necked one) and Thor (the blond one).

"I guess Celeste and Jules had to get back to their kids," I say.

"Yes," he says tightly.

I lower my voice. "Did it not go well tonight?"

"Lucas!" a feminine voice squeals. "What're you doing here, gorgeous?"

I turn to see a tall, thin, young brunette with sharp cheek-bones wearing what is no doubt a designer skin-tight pink sleeveless dress with black stilettos. Basically, the anti-Alice. We're both in pink—I'm in my pink polka-dotted dress—but the results are staggeringly different. She sounds American and looks like a model.

"Bella," he murmurs warmly.

She gives him a light hug, kissing his cheek, and then remains closer to him than I am. Her voice lowers to a sexy purr. "How long are you in town for?"

Lucas's lips curve into a slow charming smile. "Not long. Let me guess, you're here for a fashion show."

I am wallpaper.

"Close! It's a magazine shoot." She glances around the lobby. "I'm meeting my agent here for a drink." She slides her manicured pink fingernails around the side of his neck. "I'm at the Ritz. Stop by tonight."

"Hi!" I chirp. The wallpaper speaks!

Lucas startles like he forgot I existed. Bella's unnaturally green eyes—definitely contacts—widen as she takes me in for the first time. "Who are you?"

Lucas finally acknowledges me. "Um, yes, I was going to say I'm with someone tonight." He doesn't say fiancée or even my name. It shouldn't hurt as much as it does.

Pride stung, I provide the information Lucas was too gobsmacked by model beauty to impart. "I'm Alice, his fiancée."

She bursts out laughing. "Right! Who are you really? His

assistant?" She turns to Lucas, smiling like this is a fantastic joke.

Now I wish I could shrink *into* the wallpaper.

Lucas bristles. "Why is that so hard to believe? I can't have a committed relationship?" He's offended at the possibility of an insult to himself, completely missing the obvious—she thinks I'm not in his league.

She gives me a sideways look, the disdain clear on her flawless face. "She's not your usual type."

"Maybe I wanted a change," he bites out.

Which is not a compliment at all. It's an acknowledgment that I'm not in his league. Suddenly my dress seems dowdy, everything about me too awkward, nerdy, and fat. Shame swamps me, every bully's taunt bouncing around in my mind. *No! Stop the shame spiral! Be the badass!*

I find my voice. "He's spending the weekend with me, and the rest of his life, actually, so you'll need to move on, Becca."

"It's Bella," she snaps, tossing her hair.

"Whatever," I say, taking Lucas's arm and leaning against him like he's truly mine to claim. Even though I'm too pissed at him right now to actually feel affectionate, I want her gone more.

She leans close to Lucas. "Room two-oh-five if you want better." She stalks off to the bar.

I let out a shaky breath. She became every bully I ever knew and never confronted. I *am* a badass.

Lucas looks down at me. "So you do have claws."

"You're a Neanderthal, thinking with your little head."

"What did I do?" He sounds genuinely perplexed.

I speak through my teeth. "You couldn't even remember my name in the face of her perfect everything."

He smirks. "You sound jealous."

I drop my hold on his arm and put some space between us. "I'm not jealous. It's basic manners. You didn't even introduce me."

"I was surprised to see her."

"Obviously you were afflicted with model blindness."

He laughs, which irritates me further. "What is model blindness?"

I press my lips together. "You can't see anything but the model in front of you. It's a real problem with the male mind. They focus on one thing and suddenly no other female exists."

"Aww, Alice, you're so cute when you're jealous."

"I'm not cute. Not jealous either, so stop saying that." I don't want people to look at us and think he could do better, even if we are pretending. It's insulting.

"I haven't been with Bella, you know."

"Well, she sure wants to be with you." I sound peevish, and I don't care. It's basic manners, common decency that he lacked, and now he's acting like *I'm* the one with the issue.

I silently seethe. I hate that I felt invisible.

"Let's just go," he says and walks toward the door.

"Fine by me," I say, catching up to him.

The guards flank us and usher us into a limo waiting out front. Once we're settled into the backseat of the limo, I arrange my pink polka-dotted dress over my legs, smoothing it out. My brain whispers an irritated chant: *clueless man, clueless man*.

Thor is sitting adjacent to us, the perfect chaperone to the fake couple. Hercules is in the front passenger seat with the driver. Lucas pulls out his phone, texting rapidly, probably reporting back to Anna and Gabriel about his dinner meeting. Finally, he tucks the phone away, lets out a long low breath, and stretches out his legs.

"So, how did the business part go?" I ask in an attempt to move past my irritation. The business dinner was the main reason for our fake engagement, after all.

His lips press into a flat line. "Fine. It would've been better if you were there."

"I *was* there," I say through my teeth.

"Barely." There's an edge to his voice that puts me even more on edge.

"You're mad at me for being late? I did the best I could in an impossible situation, and guess what, Mr. Charming? I'm mad at *you* for treating me like I was completely invisible while that woman was all over you. And you didn't even come to my defense when she insulted me!"

He rubs the back of his neck. "Here we are, fighting like a real engaged couple. I get all the hassle and none of the benefits."

My head rears back. "Excuse me? I thought I did a pretty good job talking to Celeste, which is not easy for me with someone I just met. Newsflash, I'm an introvert. And I took the time to sign a gazillion books, each with a different inscription, so she and her friends would feel special. So don't tell me you don't get benefits!"

He arches a brow.

I gasp, realization hitting me. He means the other kind of benefits. "Gah! Men are pigs. Clueless pigs."

He studies me for a long moment. "You prefer fictional men to the real thing, don't you?"

Yes! I cross my arms. "Sometimes I do."

Silence falls. An uncomfortable, awkward silence.

Finally, Lucas speaks. "I was out of line. You did the best you could to get here. Thank you."

"You're welcome," I say as graciously as I can, given he hasn't acknowledged the invisible wallpaper thing.

"Are you still mad?"

"No." *Extremely irritated but not mad.*

He blows out a breath. "Don't give Bella another thought. I would've been with her by now if I wanted her. We go to a lot of the same parties."

I cross my legs primly. "Isn't that good to hear?"

He chuckles and tugs a lock of my hair. "Don't be jealous."

"I'm not."

"Hey, the meeting went well. Jules told me to bring the paperwork on Monday morning to the bank. I think I got it."

"Really?"

He flashes a smile so big I find myself smiling back. "Yes. And even though you weren't here as early as I would've liked, it was your belief in me that gave me a boost, so thank you for that too."

"Of course!" I know how much he wanted this. I'm so happy for him I want to reach out and hug him. At the last minute I remember myself and just wave my hands in the air. We're not playing the engagement game here in the privacy of the limo, so I'm not supposed to touch. "Yay! What were his exact words?"

He pinches my chin. "They were in French, but it was an implied likely."

"That's great. I'm so thrilled for you." And I truly am. Bella really got my back up, but if I'm being honest, it was Lucas's reaction to her that triggered my own insecurities. I shouldn't have been so upset. Lucas is my friend.

I relax, leaning my head back against the headrest. "You shocked me when you switched to French. I didn't know you spoke it."

"Our family is all bilingual because the ruling power must be in touch with its people. A lot of the islanders speak both English and French since England controlled the island and more recently France. Plus France is close by."

"Is English your first language? You're very good at it."

He nods. "My mother spoke to us in English because she learned French later in life when she married my father and isn't comfortable with it. My father spoke English to be part of the conversation. Me and my siblings had French tutors at an early age, and we frequently visited France to practice conversation."

"It's a romantic language. I might set my next trilogy here."

"So it seems our engagement has ultimately been fruitful for both of us."

"A whole fruit salad," I quip.

He chuckles. "Bon appétit!"

"I know that one! I'll add that to my French vocab. Look at me already branching out from my short menu."

He grins. "Éclair and croissant?"

"Yes, and quiche."

He takes my hand, lifting it to his lips and brushing a kiss across my knuckles. *"C'est magnifique."*

My breath stutters out. Are we back to the game, or is this real? I quickly cover with a casualness I'm far from feeling. "I like all your princely stops. And here I was thinking your princely education was lacking."

His lips curl into a crooked grin. "I picked up a few more stops in *The Duke's Dare.*"

He read my story!

My mind does a quick review through that story, though it was a while ago. The duke was supremely chivalrous and, on a dare, courted a young woman known for being a wallflower. Only he fell for her and twisted himself into knots trying to convince her of the truth of his love once she discovered she was part of a dare. There was quite a lot of groveling and worshipping at her feet before the stolen kisses and, ultimately, passion. I sigh a dreamy sigh remembering Hugh.

"Alice, where did you go?"

"Back to Hugh," I say on a sigh. "He's my fantasy man."

"Is he based on anyone?"

"Right!" I scoff. "I made him up for what men lack. Hugh holds a special place in my heart. I spent a lot of time with him in college after some less than satisfying experiences. Let's just say the men I was with before I found Hugh were more boys than men. Immature. And really insensitive."

"Ah. I think that might be the case for most university hookups."

I straighten in my seat. "Well, that's just it. I thought they were relationships after a few dates, or at least something with the potential for a relationship, but after we hooked up, I never heard from them again. In fact, they left immediately afterward with a mumbled excuse. I suppose my expectations were too high—"

"You deserve more," he says. "Better treatment than that."

I soften, feeling extremely warm toward him again. "Thank you, Lucas. It's nice of you to say so. Were you like that at university?"

"I was," he says a little sheepishly. "Maybe if I met the right woman, I wouldn't have been."

I look out the window, disappointed for some reason, even though I know his reputation. "I suppose you couldn't help it, being a guy."

"We do mature," he says.

I glance over at him. "It's really too bad that women are mature a good ten years before men. I suppose that's why I liked Mason. He was older than me by nine years and seemed to have his head on straight."

He bristles. "No comment."

He gets irritated over Mason, but I was expecting to marry him only one week ago. It's not like Mason doesn't exist for me anymore. I've been ignoring his texts and calls urging me to talk to him. I don't want to have anything to do with him, but some part of me is curious. Maybe he realized he made a mistake and wants to apologize and beg me to go back to him. It would be nice to have an apology, even if the answer is, *no way, go to hell, and take my former best friend with you*. Not bitter at all. Ha-ha. I actually am feeling a lot better now that I have my writing mojo back. In no small part due to Lucas boosting my spirits. Except for tonight's spat, I've really enjoyed his company.

When we arrive at the hotel, Lucas helps me out of the limo and then keeps my hand tucked in his as we walk. I guess now that we're in public, we're playing the game. I love it more than I should. I almost wish I could fall in love with Lucas. He really is wonderful and gorgeous and, well, Lucas. I'm just not ready to open my heart again.

He stops suddenly in front of a small puddle and makes a big production out of taking off his imaginary cape and laying it down for me. "My lady."

I burst out laughing. "Nice! That's going in my book."

He grins, takes my hand, and guides me in a wide arc around the puddle. I fill in the rest of the scene in my mind, substituting a grand ducal carriage for the limo we were just in. The luxury hotel is the duke's estate. I pretend that Thor is our chaperone, the duke's widowed aunt. Even I can't imagine thick-necked huge Hercules as the aunt, though Thor is no slouch in the muscle department. Lucas has proved endlessly inspiring. I barely have to tweak his speech to take on a more romantic tinge. The deep timbre of his voice is pure duke territory too.

A few moments later, we're all checked in at the hotel, and the guards escort us to the private elevator for the penthouse suite. The moment the doors close behind us, the guards leave, heading for their room on the floor below.

Lucas hits the button to go up.

I gulp, hyperaware of him standing next to me in his dark gray suit perfectly tailored to his large muscular build. My imagination takes a dirty dive into a middle-of-the-night seduction scene, and I flush with heat.

Think it through, Alice. He's booked a suite with *two* bedrooms, which means there are no expectations of anything remotely physical. *Overactive erotic imagination stand down!* I'm not in his league, something he acknowledged tonight and, even if I was, I'm not getting involved with someone with his kind of reputation, especially so soon after getting my heart annihilated. I probably don't even have the capability of letting anyone into my blackened heart. And, though it would be more convenient given my growing attraction to my fake fiancé here, I have never been a casual-sex kind of woman. I know that about myself. I need some emotion to go with the physical, which I'm not ready for. Not even for a fun guy like Lucas, who did apologize for his earlier misstep, who makes me laugh, and who actually took the time to read my book and emulates the hero with chival-rous gestures.

I casually shift away from temptation. I'm *not* making a move on him. I only have to think back to three days ago when I suggested a practice kiss. He was so stiff and uncomfortable I felt like a lech for suggesting it. So embarrassing. And he only gave me a kiss on the cheek tonight in front of Jules and Celeste. Obviously my romance mind is working overtime. Le sigh. Now that I'm into my new story, I have sex on the brain. It's one of my favorite scenes to write. I like to have a nice big sexy scene at the end full of love and passion that is so very satisfying.

I catch Lucas's eye in the mirrored wall of the elevator. His gaze smolders into mine. My breath catches. The hair on the back of my neck rises, every nerve ending in my body tingling to life.

I look away, my pulse kicking up, my breath coming harder. This is *not* my imagination anymore. He wants me.

10

———

"Are you tired?" he asks, breaking the sexually tense elevator silence.

Do not pass go. Do not hook up with the world's most eligible royal bachelor.

I nod vigorously and fake a yawn. "It's been quite a day, and that cognac really relaxed me."

He rubs the back of his neck, glancing sideways at me. "I might stay up for a bit."

"Sure. Whatever you like."

Silence falls, and it's more than a little uncomfortable. It's downright awkward now like I said the wrong thing. Maybe he expects me to fall at his feet like every other woman on the planet.

"What will you do?" I ask, playing the casual friendly conversation game. I'm going straight to bed and staying there. Alone.

"Probably watch some TV. See if a movie is on."

"What kind of movie?"

"The kind they play in French hotel rooms," he snaps. "I don't know."

I stiffen at his tone. "It was just a question. Geez. I don't care what you watch."

"Sorry," he mumbles.

The elevator doors open, and he gestures for me to go ahead. I grab my wheeled suitcase, but he says, "I've got it."

"Thank you," I murmur and walk ahead to the door.

He uses his key card and holds the door to the suite open for me. Another nice chivalrous gesture. The light is on for us, and I step into a spacious living room done in a modern style with a leather sofa, flat-screen TV, and geometric-patterned rug. Toward the back of the room, I spot a small kitchen. French doors on opposite sides of the living room open to the bedrooms. Perfect. I probably won't even notice he's here, sleeping on opposite sides of the suite.

I turn to him about to say goodnight, when he goes to check out the near bedroom and then heads across the way to the other one.

"I'll take whichever one you don't want," I call. "I'm not picky."

He returns, grabs my suitcase, and deposits it in the far bedroom. Okay, guess that one is mine. I join him in my bedroom, taking in the giant king-size bed all done in white with an abundance of cushy pillows.

His jaw is clenched, tension held in the set of his shoulders. "I gave you the one with the better view."

I admit to feeling a little happy that he desires me (at least I think that's what's going on). He's holding himself in check and irritated about it because he's a man used to getting what he wants when he wants it. If he is restraining himself, that's a princely thing to do. I could be wrong, though. I'm not sure how to explain our stiff-as-cardboard practice kiss if he actually wants me. Maybe I grew on him? Maybe he turned down Bella and now he's revved up with nowhere to go? All I know for sure is I'm not going there.

"Thanks, Lucas, for everything. You've been really good to me, and I appreciate it."

"Right. Goodnight." He leaves, shutting the double doors

behind him, effectively shutting me away before I can get out my own goodnight.

"Goodnight!" I call through the door belatedly.

I get ready for bed, changing into my favorite sleep shirt that reads So Many Books So Little Time with my pale blue sleep shorts. I hear the TV go on in the living room and tell myself to stay put.

My self doesn't listen, and I pull open the door and poke my head out. He's not in there. The doors to his bedroom are closed. Maybe he's getting ready for bed too. Is he one of those men who strip down to their boxer briefs when they get comfortable at night? I will *not* sneak a peek.

This is silly. I really am tired, and I want to be well rested for sightseeing tomorrow. I won't be back here anytime soon.

I climb into bed and turn off the light.

Lucas

I'm restless, tense, and I know exactly why, but I don't want it to be that because then I've screwed this whole thing up. It was supposed to be a game. I mean, yes, I was attracted to her from the first time we met, but I also felt protective. She's in a vulnerable place and not over her ex. I told myself not to get too close, but now that I've gotten to know her... she's bright and quick-witted and so fucking sexy. I have never once been bored in her presence, and that's no small thing. The pull to her is stronger than I'm used to with a woman, beyond desire to raging need. She checks every box for what I like in a woman, and I had the lousy luck to meet her at the worst possible time in her life.

I stalk out to the living room to watch TV, barely noticing what's on. I turned it on earlier so I'd stop listening to Alice getting ready, and imagining what she looked like naked. For a brief moment earlier tonight, when Alice had a jealous snit over Bella, it actually felt like the fiancée thing was real, like Alice wanted me all to herself because she cared. I didn't introduce Alice because I knew Bella wouldn't be kind. She never is with other women.

I blow out a frustrated breath, too wired even to sit on the sofa. Playing at fiancé was supposed to be easy. What am I supposed to do with this craving to be near her? To feel her softness pressed against me? I stare at her closed bedroom doors.

This is so stupid. She's right there, yet she might as well be back in Oregon because I can't be the asshole here. She deserves better and, if I act on these urges, this whole thing will blow up in my face. Drama with a capital D. I know it. And then it will bring unwanted attention to us, especially from Anna and Gabriel. They don't know I went forward with the fake-engagement plan.

I turn off the TV and go to my bedroom, climbing into bed.

A few restless minutes later, I throw back the covers, heading for the shower. Time for a date with my hand. I'm barely started when images of Alice flash through my mind —her shy smile, her laugh, her hand on my arm, her fantastic breasts. Fuck. Anyone else. I search my mind desperately, but there she is again, only this time she's wearing the pink lacey sheer lingerie she showed me. It's like a movie in my mind so vividly real my breathing accelerates. Time slows down, and then I'm gone. The release is a relief.

But when I lean my forehead against the shower wall, catching my breath, I'm unsatisfied. I need more. I need Alice.

What did I get myself into?

I have to protect her, and the only way to do that is to keep my distance.

∿

Alice

After a good night's sleep, I'm positive I did the right thing keeping my distance from the temptation that is Lucas.

He's not a staying kind of guy, and I'm not ready even if he was. I will proceed on a friendly course from now on. I need coffee to crank start my brain in the morning, but I'm just vain enough to brush the bedhead look from my hair and brush my teeth before peeking out of the bedroom.

"Good morning," Lucas says, surprising me. He's standing in the living room looking at me expectantly, already freshly showered and dressed in a short-sleeved light blue collared shirt, tailored tan pants, and loafers. I don't think he owns a T-shirt or shorts. It's a little disconcerting to find him wide awake and waiting for me. How long has he been standing there?

"Morning," I say, stepping out of the room. I sniff the air, sensing caffeine. "Did you make coffee?" I look toward the kitchen but don't see any.

His voice is gruff. "What are you wearing?"

I glance down at my sleep shirt. "Pajamas." It's a long shirt and shorts, not even remotely sexy.

He stares at the hem of my shirt and gestures at me. "Is there something under there?"

"Under where?" I grin at my little underwear joke, lifting the shirt to show him. He backs up a step, looking away. "Relax, it's shorts. Have you been waiting for me long?"

"A bit. I ordered us some breakfast." He gestures to the round table in front of the sofa.

I join him on the sofa, and he pours me a cup of coffee before taking a seat next to me. "Thanks."

He's extremely solicitous, offering me a basket full of croissants and muffins. I take a chocolate croissant. There's also fruit slices, cheese, and a couple of hard-boiled eggs.

"This was really thoughtful," I say. "Thanks so much. Are you going to eat too?"

His gaze is glued to where my sleep shirt ends and my bare leg begins. "I ate," he says hoarsely.

I take a fortifying sip of coffee, ignoring the possible desire in his voice. "Did you sleep okay?"

"Fine. You?"

"Can't complain. I'm glad I slept in a bit. I was up late reading."

He frowns. "I thought you were tired last night."

"I was, but I always read before bed. It's very addicting. You get to the end of a chapter and you just have to keep going to find out what happens next. I've got a whole library on my phone so I always have something to read." I take a bite of warm croissant and moan in appreciation.

Lucas leaps up, looking around frantically.

My eyes widen, suddenly awake. "What's wrong?"

"I'm the good guy here," he mutters before heading to his room.

"Of course you're a good guy!" I call reassuringly. Gabriel must really be doing a number on his self-esteem. "You're great! Just look at how you've been so chivalrous with all the princely manners. And thoughtful too."

Silence.

I sip more delicious coffee and take another bite of croissant, watching his doorway to see what surprising thing he'll do next.

He appears a moment later, leaning casually with one arm against the door frame. "I am pretty great."

I smile, glad he's sounding back to normal. "Damn right you are. Oh no! We forgot to celebrate how great you are last night with champagne!"

He steps closer. "I was distracted by my victory."

"C'mere, we'll toast with orange juice. Oh, wait, is this a mimosa? Perfect!"

He returns to the living room, picks up a mimosa, and stands across the table from where I'm sitting. I stand and offer a toast. "To the new CFO."

His eyes are intent on mine. "To my fiancée."

I choke on my own spit. "That sounded real. We don't have to pretend when it's just the two of us. Maybe change it to a toast to our friendship. Honestly, I don't know how I would've gotten through this week without you. To new friends."

He looks pensive for a moment, and I think maybe he's going to add something heartfelt about our friendship, but then he just clinks his glass to mine and drinks.

I take a seat and go back to eating.

He sits next to me. "How're you feeling?"

I lift my coffee mug up to him in a gesture of appreciation. "Beginning to feel human again."

"Are you still…um, heartbroken?"

I get serious. "That will take some time to heal." I attempt a smile, but it feels wobbly. "I'm really trying to move forward. I think some sightseeing is just the distraction I need." I pick at a buttery layer of croissant, sober now.

"Do you want to know what I've planned, or should I surprise you?"

I refocus on him. His blue-green eyes are sparkling like he has something really fantastic planned. I clasp my hands together as a truly exciting possibility occurs to me. "Are we going to a royal ball?"

"Close. There aren't any happening during the time you're here. I did check, but they're not as common as they once were." A smile tugs at his lips like he's eager to share. "You might think this is even better. We're taking a private tour of Versailles."

I gasp. Versailles is a famous palatial estate, the former royal residence of Louis XIV. It is *legendary*.

He goes on. "We'll be there during the musical fountain show this afternoon, and tonight we'll attend the ball held there exactly as they would have during the Baroque era. It's my way of thanking you for your support on the business side. I hope it will inspire your story."

"Yes," I breathe. "I didn't even know they had musical fountain shows or a ball there."

He grins. "They do in the summer."

"And the fountains are, like, the original seventeenth-century fountains?"

"The very same with Baroque music in the background."

I blink. It's history nerd nirvana.

He leans close. "The ball is in the Hall of Mirrors."

"Get out!" I shove his shoulder with both hands, and he laughs. I clap a hand over my mouth. I've seen pictures of the Hall of Mirrors. It's so much more than a hall. It's an outrageously gilded vaulted room that can take your breath away, even in pictures. The ceiling is hand-painted with numerous military and political victories. Large windows run along one side, and on the other side, arches feature hundreds of gilded mirrors (a luxury at the time). Crystal chandeliers, gold trim, marble statues, inlaid hardwood floor, gold, so much glittery shiny gold. "We're going to a ball *there*?"

"Yes," he says on a laugh. "A good surprise, then?"

I look down at my pajamas and meet his eyes. "I don't have a formal dress."

"We'll shop for one today. I heard they may have a few women's clothing shops in Paris."

I'm speechless. A prince is buying me a formal dress in Paris and taking me to a ball in a historic famous hall. It's ringing all of my bells—I'm talking orgasmic levels—princely gesture, fashion, a ball set in a historical time in a historical place. I'm beside myself.

He takes my hand, admiring the ruby engagement ring he gave me, his voice husky. "Maybe a dress to go with your ring."

"Yes. You're so...amazing." I stare at his large hand holding mine, and then lift my gaze to his. My breath stalls at the heat in his eyes, my lips parting as desire unfurls within me. The urge to close the distance overwhelms me, and I shift the tiniest bit closer, unable to resist.

He slowly pulls away and releases my hand. "I'm glad I chose well." Does he mean today's outing or me? Do I want it to be me?

He walks over to the window, looking out at the view. I join him with my coffee, admiring the city from up so high. It's a gorgeous sunny day shining down on lots of cute houses and a cathedral in the distance. I'm in the City of

Lights, the most romantic place on Earth, with a gorgeous prince who hits all my buttons.

My certainty of the friendly path with Lucas wavers. Do I dare risk it?

What would a badass do?

11

<hr>

Alice

By the time I'm ready for our day, dressed in a cute light blue short-sleeved tunic with white leggings and my favorite black glitter Keds sneakers, Lucas is back to the game, all charm and gallant behavior. It's so fun pretending I have a besotted fiancé. My own real-life fiancé admittedly never came close to my romance-hero dreams. Probably Lucas wouldn't either if I hadn't specifically asked him to. It helps that he basically read my playbook by reading *The Duke's Dare*. That story was my fantasy played out during a very unsatisfying college dating period. Imagine if my ex had made that kind of effort!

Our first order of business is finding me a formal dress for the ball tonight. He opens the door for me to a boutique with an enchanting collection of cocktail dresses and gowns. Lucas and the guards stand off to one side, looking impossibly manly and out of place in the feminine shop. I've never shopped with three men before. The saleswoman, a blonde in her fifties with severely sharp cheekbones, wearing a green A-line dress, greets us in French and leaves me to browse.

Within minutes, I've come to the embarrassing conclusion

that women in Paris must be much smaller than me, because the sizes stop at ten.

I glance at Lucas waiting patiently for me to choose something, and then at the saleswoman. I'm about to tell Lucas I can make do with the dress I have when the saleswoman says pointedly to me in heavily accented English, "Perhaps try another shop for women like you."

I nod jerkily, my cheeks burning.

Lucas fires back in French, and the clerk says something in a disdainful tone, waving her hand dismissively at me.

My gut churns. I'm so embarrassed I can't think straight. All I know is I need to get out of here. I give Lucas's arm a tug. "Let's just go."

"Yes, we'll try a better shop," he says. "This one has gone downhill." He adds something in French that sounds like *kiss off*.

The moment we step outside, I blurt, "We can skip shopping. I can make do."

"Too late," he says, guiding me to a shop two doors down. "You wanted to go to a ball, so you need a gown."

"But—"

"Stop arguing, darling. We're supposed to be happily engaged."

He opens the door to the next shop, his hand on my lower back pushing me firmly inside. I'm still flushed with embarrassment and unsure how to deal with the size issue. There must be at least one plus-size woman in Paris, right? I can't bring myself to discuss it with Lucas, drawing his attention to my body shape. Sure, he appreciates my breasts, all men find them fascinating, but most men seem to prefer more of a stick shape to hold them up. The guards remain stone-faced witnesses in the background, and I force myself not to add in their internal dialogue over this mortifying situation. Yes, I've reached mortification levels. If this shop doesn't work out, I am running back to the hotel, back to my trusty laptop with its genteel Regency world, where dresses are custom made to fit perfectly.

Hell, if this goes worse than the last place, I might run all the way back to Oregon. I don't care if there's an ocean in the way.

A saleswoman approaches, a young brunette wearing a stylish asymmetrical white dress that clings to her skinny body. This is never going to work. I take a step back, knocking into the solid form of Hercules. "Sorry!"

He gives a slight incline of his head, but is otherwise silent.

Lucas takes over, speaking to the saleswoman in rapid French. She responds cordially, glancing at my ruby engagement ring before smiling and gesturing for me to follow her.

A small flame of hope gives me the confidence to attempt another try. She produces a red empire waist gown with cute off-the-shoulder cap sleeves that looks promising. I take it to the dressing room and manage to get it on, but there's just no room to breathe the way it clings to my rib cage.

"Lucas?" I call.

A moment later, he's speaking through the door. "Do you like it?"

"Yes, but I can't breathe in it."

"Let me see."

I squinch my eyes tight, about to tell him *forget it*, when he says in a husky voice, "Darling, you could make a sack look good."

I find myself smiling, even though I know he's just playing the game. He's my besotted fiancé and would never utter a harsh word to me.

I open the door.

His gaze rakes me from head to toe before slowly lifting to my eyes. I try not to fidget, waiting for the verdict. I hoped he'd say a quick, "If you like it, I like it," which is the dialogue I would've created for him. And then I would say, "You know, I don't care for it after all. Let's just go." And this whole embarrassing awkward time would mercifully end.

"Never mind," I blurt.

"I like it," he says hoarsely.

The hoarseness in his voice makes me feel a little better. It's a sexy sound of wanting and restraint. "Oh. Well, I do too, but I also like to breathe." I run my hands down my rib cage. "I have to breathe shallowly. I'd rather not need a fainting couch."

He looks serious, completely ignoring my attempt to lighten the situation with Regency humor. "I'll fix it. Give me a minute."

I watch as he returns to the saleswoman, barking out French like he's Napoleon himself (but much taller). He. Is. Magnificent.

Next thing I know I'm standing in an open space of the dressing room area in front of a three-way mirror in my regular clothes while the saleswoman measures me just about everywhere you can measure. I meet Lucas's eyes in the mirror. "Are they tailoring the gown for me?"

"Yes, and it will be delivered to our hotel room this afternoon."

"Wow. I should always bring you shopping with me."

He makes a courtly bow. I'm about to laugh at how over the top the gesture is, but he looks so serious when he straightens, his eyes heated and locked on mine in the mirror, that the laugh goes right out of me. Sparks fire over my skin. My God, he hasn't even touched me. I'm burning up.

By the time we finish our shopping and climb into the waiting limo for our drive to Versailles, something is off with Lucas. He's tense and quiet. I'd like to think it's the strain of resisting me, but my mind fills in much worse. He's tense because he had to deal with the hassle of shopping and tailoring stuff. Or he's not enjoying the game anymore. Or maybe he doesn't want to indulge me this weekend doing all my nerdy history things. He's used to a much faster-paced partying lifestyle. I don't want him to feel forced into being my besotted fiancé, going shopping, and doing nerdy historic stuff. On the other hand, wasn't that our deal? I play fiancée for his banker meeting, and he plays fiancé to inspire my story? This ball is the perfect experience to drop into my story. I'm torn between letting him off the hook and demanding he get back to our deal. I can't take all this quiet tension.

I lean close to whisper to him because Thor is in the back of the limo with us. "Are we still playing the engagement game?"

He speaks under his breath, looking straight ahead. "Do you want to?"

"Yes, but I wonder if you're enjoying it? You seem tense."

He remains quiet, tense, and serious.

I let him off the hook. I don't want him to play the part if it's going to be like this. "You don't have to."

He meets my eyes, his gaze intense. "I want to."

"Oh." I think on that for a moment, confused. "I'm missing something here, then. What's wrong?"

"Nothing. I just need some time to get into sightseeing. I've got a lot on my mind."

But he seemed cheerful this morning. That is, until we went shopping. I relax. "Ohhh, guys don't like shopping. That's what it is. Now you'll have more fun."

"I don't mind. I liked seeing you in that gown, even if you couldn't breathe."

"You want me to faint at the ball?" I ask in mock anger.

His lips curve into a crooked smile. "I would catch you."

I smile back, pleased we're getting back to our normal banter. "I can totally picture that! And then he carries her off to a private alcove, where he wakes her from her swoon with a kiss." My mind carries the scene forward. "She's terribly compromised. When they return to the ball, there are witnesses that saw them go off alone together. They *must* marry, or she'll be ruined, her reputation in tatters."

"You're writing out loud again," he says in a teasing voice. "Your voice gets dreamy and a little bit British."

"What? I don't do a British accent!"

He grins and says, "Maybe it's just your Regency-style word choice. You certainly don't sound American."

"How funny! I had no idea." At least Mason never

commented on it. Of course, we didn't live together. We planned to after the wedding, but he didn't like any of the places we looked at and finally said I could just move in to his apartment when the time came. It hits me that he wasn't just being picky, he was trying to decide between going through with our wedding or jumping ship for Riley. Mason dragging his feet should've been a red flag. Why couldn't this all have been clear back then? I wouldn't have been so blindsided.

"Alice?"

"Huh?"

"I said I like hearing you write out loud. It's adorable."

My cheeks flush. "Oh."

He takes my hand, entwining our fingers together, a more intimate hold than before when he simply tucked my hand in his. I still, looking straight ahead, my heart pounding because this feels like real affection and desire together, my personal relationship trigger, and I'm *this close* to freaking out.

I don't know what to do or say. I can enjoy myself when I know the parameters of the game, but things are getting fuzzy, and it's making me very nervous. I don't think Lucas would mean to hurt me but, ultimately, he would. Because he would walk away easily, on to the next woman. And my barely pieced together heart would be shattered beyond repair.

Calm down. He's just holding your hand.

Lucas looks over at me, studying my expression. "What?"

I stare down at our entwined fingers, my ruby engagement ring sparkling up at me. I keep my voice low. "Are we holding hands because of the game?"

"It's making you uncomfortable." He releases my hand.

"I'm sorry. I feel...I don't know. It's kind of weird and confusing. I'm sure it's just because of Mason being—"

"No problem." He shifts his body away from me, looking out the window.

I hope I didn't screw up. I was being honest, speaking up about my feelings in a way I rarely do with a man.

I miss his touch already.

12

Lucas

I'm acting weird and making her uncomfortable. This is a first. I'm known for being smooth and charming, yet with Alice I'm as awkward as an adolescent. And I wasn't even awkward then! It's this damn attraction. This would be so much easier if I wasn't drawn in by her soft feminine sexy *everything*. My God, her voice, her scent, her lush body. It's driving me insane. I'm seriously considering taking the jet back to Villroy, skipping the whole sightseeing thing, and then flying back solo on Monday for my meeting, but one look at Alice's excitement as we pull up to Versailles has me taking it all back.

"Wow, wow, wow!" she exclaims. "It's huge!"

I've seen it before, but I try to see it with new eyes. It's a three-story immense chateau with a series of repeating windows across the front. The perfect symmetry of the windows is broken up by multiple Ionic columns and statues. I tell her what I know about it. "It once was the seat of French royalty and government. It's so immense—more than two thousand rooms—you can't get the whole thing into a picture. Baroque architecture in all its lavish extravagance."

She lets out a little squeal and rushes out of the limo,

snapping pictures with her phone despite what I just told her about it being too big to get into a picture.

I catch up to her, the guards following close behind, and follow her through the large courtyard as she marvels. Her open enjoyment warms my heart. I can't believe I almost bailed on her. What a shit move that would've been. Obviously I'm not cut out for relationships, only thinking of myself.

She turns to me, her voice eager. "Let's see the inside now."

"Right this way." I gesture toward the visitors' door. Once inside, I lead the way to the information desk, where I check in for our private tour.

Alice's blue eyes are huge as she whispers, "I can't believe we get the private tour!"

"It's because I'm Prince Lucas Rourke," I whisper back with a straight face.

She smiles her sweet smile, and my heart kicks up. It gets me every time. "I know who you are. I guess I'm just not used to the VIP treatment."

I am. It's great most of the time, and other times I wish I could just blend and go about my life. I keep that to myself. "I hope you enjoy it, darling," I say instead, rather gallantly.

"I shall," she says with a grin.

A short while later, we go on our tour, heading through a reserved entrance and stepping into the splendor of the king's private apartments. Our tour continues to the rest of the royals' apartments, their private chapel, the main apartments, and the royal opera house. Alice is beside herself, oohing and ahhing through the tour, occasionally grabbing my arm in her excitement. Everything feels fresh through her eyes. Though it still feels over the top with all the gold fabrics, heavy marbling, and high domes. We finish the tour in the Hall of Mirrors, where we'll be attending the ball later tonight.

She turns to me, her blue eyes bright. "I can't believe we're going to a ball here! In this very room!" Her brows knit together. "Are we supposed to know some Baroque dance moves?"

"I have no idea. I've never attended a Baroque ball. I think we'll be safe with the standard waltz."

She grimaces. "I've never waltzed either."

"It's easy. I'll lead, you just follow and try not to step on my feet."

She presses a hand to her forehead. "Why didn't I think of this? I should've Googled Baroque dancing."

"Relax. I'll show you right now." I take her hand and place my other hand in the center of her back for better control. "It's a simple box step. For you, it's right foot back, then left foot joins it. Then to the side and feet together. Ready?"

She blushes prettily. "Okay." I'm not sure if it's me being close or the fact that our tour guide and the guards are watching us. I hope it's the first.

I do a slow box step, using my hand to guide her with me. She follows beautifully, her eyes on our feet.

"Hey, I'm pretty good at this," she says, looking up at me and crunching my toe in the process. I suppress a wince, not wanting to discourage her. "Oops! Sorry." She pulls away. "I'll practice a bit in the room before tonight. Let's go see the gardens."

I let out a breath of disappointment. The gardens are more enticing than dancing with me. I must be losing my touch.

The gardens are formal, impressive in their grandeur, including a grand canal with gondolas and numerous fountains. Alice is so excited she's practically running from one section to the next. She holds up her brochure. "There's fifty-five fountains and one hundred fifty-five statues. We have to see them all!"

I can't help but delight in her clear enjoyment of everything. We finish our tour with a stop at a small cart for lunch and take in the musical fountain show. When it ends, she leans over and kisses my cheek just above my beard. "What a wonderful treat. Thanks so much for bringing me here."

"My pleasure."

"Let's head back. I want to have time to freshen up and practice dancing."

I do one of my formal bows. See? I had some princely education. "As you wish, my dear Alice."

She beams, her cheeks coloring with pink. She puts her hands to her cheeks. "I don't know if this is because you read my book or the game, but I am *loving* it!"

Unfortunately, so am I. Her pleasure is my pleasure. I don't even mind making an ass of myself with the bows and such because all I care about is her reaction.

She falls asleep on my shoulder on the drive back. I smooth her soft hair away from her face. Two things strike me at the same time—I'm looking forward to the ball tonight, and I'm dreading its end because I don't think I can resist her for a second night in a shared hotel suite.

Alice

Tonight is magical. I can hardly believe I'm here in the freaking Hall of Mirrors, the most famous historic room in the world with its over-the-top opulence, wearing a gown tailored to my exact measurements with a handsome prince in a tux. Pinch me!

We already enjoyed some refreshments—champagne and strawberries, to be precise—and toasted each other over last night's successful business meeting. Now we're dancing a waltz alongside other couples. There's probably a hundred people here in formal wear, seeming to delight in the historic ball as much as I am. It's heaven for a history nerd. The best part is that Lucas is such a fantastic lead, I can spend all my time ogling the room and the other couples. This is all going in my book.

Lucas turns us, pressing me closer as he does. My focus is abruptly torn from the luxurious room to the fact that there is no polite distance between us anymore. Now there's miniscule space. The heat of him warms my front, and everything else fades in my mind. There is only me and Lucas.

"You've improved since this afternoon," he says with a crooked smile. "My feet haven't been stepped on more than five times. That's progress."

"Hey! I think it was only twice."

He winks. "Tell that to my toes."

I shake my head. "Sorry. You're a wonderful dancer."

His warm tender smile takes my breath away. "Thank you, my darling."

I lick my lips and stare blindly at a point over his shoulder. I need to focus on the purpose of tonight, inspiration for my story. That's what that *darling* was about. He's playing a part for me. "Would it be weird if I took pictures?"

"Go ahead."

"I will, after our dance. Then as soon as we're done here, I'm going straight to my laptop before I forget a single detail. I'm definitely setting my next trilogy here in France. Maybe it will feature someone in the French nobility who's a frequent visitor to Versailles."

"We might be here late. There're professional dancers later performing for us in period costume. I've heard it feels like you stepped back in time."

"Eeep! Okay, I get so excited I tend to rush. I'll save the writing for tomorrow morning. Then, if you don't mind, I'd like to do some more sightseeing after that. Then the next day is your bank meeting. Do you want me to go with you to that?"

"Not necessary."

I try to keep the disappointment from my voice. "It seems my use as a fake fiancée is just about up." The clock strikes midnight and Cinderella goes back to her humdrum life.

"Jules did mention they'd want to tour Villroy's spa and manufacturing area. You should be there for that as my fiancée."

"Oh. When's that?"

"I don't know. Hopefully soon."

"As long as it's in the next five weeks, we're golden."

"I'm sure it will be. Maybe even this coming week after my meeting."

The song ends, and he pulls away, still holding my hand and tucking it into the crook of his arm as he escorts me off the dance floor. Another couple immediately approaches to talk to him, and I'm reminded that he's sort of a celebrity. They're speaking in French until he pulls me closer, his hand on my lower back, to introduce me in English as his fiancée. He's trying to make me feel included after our little tiff over the lack of introduction in front of model Bella.

"Hello," I say with a smile. "So nice to meet you."

The couple smiles and nods at me, murmuring French, which I choose to think means congratulations on your engagement. I don't know.

The next hour is like that. We dance (and I get turned-on despite the fact that Lucas keeps a polite distance), and then when the dance ends, people approach him. I suppose it's the first time he's been here at a ball, and he's a bit of a novelty. I can feel myself closing up inside; the disparity between his life and status and mine is stark. Which is a shame. It's really quite romantic with the candlelight and the dancing. If only I could just enjoy it for what it is and not overthink it.

I let out a sigh as Lucas leads me to some refreshing lemonade. As soon as we're finished drinking it, he surprises me by taking my hand and pulling me directly into a private alcove at the far end of the room. The guards hover nearby, so it's never completely private.

"What are you doing?" I ask, breathless from our quick departure. Or maybe it's that I'm here with him.

He steps close, brushing my hair back behind my ear in a tender gesture that makes my heart hammer. His gaze searches mine. "Are you tired of the ball? We can leave."

My breath quickens. "No, I love it."

"Alice, I haven't seen one smile from you in an hour."

My jaw goes slack. "You count how many times I smile?"

"I notice them." He gives a lock of my hair a tug, his smile boyishly charming. "They make me happy."

I blink, completely thrown by this incredibly romantic-sounding thing. "Why do my smiles make you happy?"

"Because I remember how sad you were when we first met."

I frown and lower my gaze, disappointed. He's pitying me. I was a mess then, and he's only been trying to cheer me up.

He tips my chin up. "Your smiles make my heart beat faster."

I gasp. It's so poetic, so romantic. "They do?"

"Yes."

"Why?"

"I don't know why. Maybe because I like to see you happy." His thumb brushes over my lower lip, and shock ripples through me at the intimate touch. "You have a very sweet smile."

The air buzzes between us, the blood rushing through my veins.

"Have you ever been engaged before?" I blurt.

"No."

"You're very good at it. I'm enjoying it so much more than my real engagement. Probably because you're pretending to be so besotted with me." *Tell me if it's real.*

His brows lower. "Your real fiancé wasn't besotted with you?"

I don't even laugh at his use of my *besotted* word because it's just sad. My real fiancé should've been besotted with me. "At first I thought he was. He was very attentive and, you know, there were the love poems."

He scowls. "The confetti."

"Yes, but with you, it's...nice." I swallow hard. "I guess you live up to your charming world's most eligible royal bachelor reputation." He scoffs, and I backtrack immediately, "Not that your rep is all there is to you. You're one of the lucky ones to have both charm and substance."

He steps closer, his voice silky. "Not everyone sees that."

My body hums in anticipation. "I see that."

He pulls me into his arms, his lips brushing my ear before he whispers, "Thank you, Alice, for seeing me."

My knees go weak, desire unfurling within me. I can feel all of him, my softness pressed against his hardness. The heat of him, his intoxicating manly scent. I want him, I truly do, and my body doesn't seem to care that my heart is still rattling around in my chest in pieces.

I have to ask. "Are we still playing the game?"

"No."

I lift my gaze to his, my heart in my throat. "What does that mean?"

"I don't know."

I look away. I don't know either. I'm beyond confused and frustrated for some reason. I'm not sure if my frustration is aimed at him or me. We're not playing a game, yet neither of us knows what that means. Someone should know. This is getting complicated and messy. I don't want to deal with complicated and messy.

I step away and take a deep breath, which does nothing to calm me. "I'm so tense right now."

He turns me so my back is to his front and brushes my hair over my shoulder, letting his fingers trail lightly over my skin in a hot shivery path. Then he places his warm hands on my bare shoulders and leans close, his voice a deep rumble in my ear. "How about a massage?"

"It's most improper," I breathe.

I can hear the smile in his voice. "We're in a private spot."

The words tumble from my lips in a heated breathy rush. "Ravish me."

"What?"

I clear my throat delicately. "I said massage me."

He does, working along my shoulders and then to the back of my neck. It is decadent. I nearly melt against him in the near orgasmic pleasure of it. He finishes, trailing his hand down my spine in a light tingling path that ends just short of my ass. My breath shudders out.

He squeezes the nape of my neck and whispers directly in my ear, "How's that?"

I'm relaxed and vibrating with tension at the same time. I whirl to face him. "Do you remember when the duke found Lady Amelia on the back balcony?" It's *The Duke's Dare*, and I want him to be daring.

Heat flares in his eyes. "I do."

My mouth goes dry. I can hardly believe my own daring. "Maybe we could play that game."

He gives me his crooked sexy smile. "We haven't even kissed yet."

"Yes, we have."

He slowly shakes his head, a hint of amusement in his eyes. "That was me resisting you." He slowly leans down, his hand cupping the back of my neck. "This is a kiss."

I stop breathing. His lips brush across mine, sending a zing through me. It's the genteel kiss of a nobleman that makes me long for more. And then he does it again, another gentle brush of his lips before he pulls back, his gaze searching mine.

I stare back in a dreamy daze, my knees wobbly. He glances down at my hand clutching his shirt over his chest. I didn't even realize I was doing that. I release my hold, smoothing his shirt down, and then I let my hands roam all over his heated chest. I barely resist the urge to rip his shirt open with both hands to see the spectacular chest I'm feeling.

My voice comes out breathy, urgent. "Now we kissed. Ravish me."

He glances around. "Here?"

The music starts up again, louder this time, along with an announcement in French. I freeze. What am I doing asking Lucas to ravish me here in public at Versailles? I am not the heroine in one of my stories, no matter how much I wish I were sometimes.

He takes my hand, his voice gentle. "Come on, the announcement said the professional dance troupe is here."

I scrunch my nose. "Could you tell I chickened out?"

His lips curve into that crooked smile that reaches in and squeezes my heart. "Yes."

"Are you disappointed?"

"No."

"Why not?" I huff indignantly. "I proposed something very carnal and now it's off the table. Isn't that something a man finds disappointing?" *Be disappointed like I am, dammit! Why couldn't I be as daring as my heroine?*

His arm bands around my waist, drawing me close again, his voice lowering to a husky drawl. "Because I know everything I need to know. There's more to come."

I shiver with excitement, pushing down every anxious worry in my mind. He wants me, and I want him. That's the only thing that matters. This moment. There is no tomorrow.

13

_____

Alice

Lucas has asked Thor to follow us in a separate car, which is provided magically by someone on staff at the ball. This is the power of celebrity.

I join Lucas in the back of the limo, note the divider separating the front seat from the backseat is up, and throw myself at him. He's just as eager, his fingers spearing through my hair, his mouth devouring mine. Sweet Jesus. It's better than my stories, better than my naughty imagination, and I didn't think that was possible.

"Alice," he murmurs, his lips trailing a hot tingling path along the line of my jaw and then along the side of my neck, his beard rubbing deliciously against my sensitive skin. "I've been wanting this, wanting you."

"Me too," I gasp out as his teeth close over the cord of my neck.

His large hands slide down my bare shoulders, my arms, my sides and then back up to cup my breasts. He flicks his finger across my nipple and it beads instantly, aching for him. He shifts the bodice of my gown down and groans, muttering, "Beautiful," and I feel beautiful with him. He makes quick work of my strapless bra and then kisses each breast almost reverently.

I slide my hand into his hair, my other hand holding him to me as his lips close around my nipple, drawing it deep into his mouth. An intense throbbing between my legs follows, and I moan long and low. I'm hot and wet and restless, desperate to get closer, to feel him pressed hard against me.

He shifts to the other breast, lavishing the same treatment on it. Pleasure shoots through me, lighting up every nerve ending, my hips moving restlessly.

"Lucas," I half groan.

He lifts his head and reclaims my mouth in a passionate kiss, lowering me under him on the long bench seat. He breaks the kiss just long enough to slide my gown up to my waist and then returns, settling himself between my legs, bringing an intense aching pleasure at the touch. It's a relief and an urging for more at the same time. The intensity of his kiss ramps up as his hips grind against me, bringing more pleasure through my silky thin panties. A rush of heat centers on that one spot he's sliding back and forth over, the friction exactly what I need. I grab his ass, keeping him close, and then I tense, everything in me coiled tight, my nails digging into him. I'm so close. I've never gotten there this easily, this quickly. Oh God.

He breaks the kiss and whispers in my ear, "Go ahead. Let go." And then he does something even more wonderful, shifting off me just enough for his fingers to slide between us. He shoves my panties aside and strokes me. The sudden direct contact sends me flying over the edge with a harsh cry, my hips moving rhythmically as he gentles his touch, drawing it out. *Yesss.*

Finally, I'm spent. I open my eyes to find him staring into mine. I'm suddenly self-conscious. "I don't usually…"

He slides his fingers into his mouth, those same fingers that were just stroking me, and sucks. A pulse throbs between my legs. I grab his head and kiss him again. I'm out of control. I need, I need, I need.

I go for the button on his pants, but he stops me, clamping a hand on my wrist. "What?" I ask, confused.

"I'm not prepared," he says hoarsely.

I run my fingers over his hard length through his pants, drawing a very satisfying groan from him. "You feel very prepared."

He eases himself off me and pulls me upright. "Not prepared with a condom."

"Oh. I'm on the pill."

Our gazes collide, the air charged between us.

"I'm clean," he says.

"Me too. My ex used a condom with me because he didn't trust that I would remember to take the pill regularly." I shrug. "I can space sometimes when I'm on a book deadline."

He closes his eyes.

I wince. "Sorry. Total buzzkill bringing up my ex. I was just trying to explain how clean I am too. Kiss me."

His lips form a flat line. "Have you ever missed a pill?"

I run my hands over his chest before working on the buttons of his shirt. "No, actually, I take it at the same time every morning."

"Your ex…fuck. Why did you stay on the pill if he used a condom? He wanted double protection?"

"No." My cheeks heat, and I stop unbuttoning his shirt, take my glasses off, and let him go out of focus. "This is getting personal."

He cradles my jaw, lifting my gaze to his, and he's so close I can see the intensity in his eyes perfectly. "So is sex," he growls. "I know what you sound like when you come. I know what you taste like."

I get hotter and wetter at his words. The intensity burning in his eyes is searing. I can't seem to find my voice. I don't want to talk about my personal stuff. I just want to get back to the sexy action.

"Answer me," he commands.

"I don't remember quite so much conversation involved

with sex," I say softly. "But, um, I stayed on the pill because it keeps my severe cramps manageable." I risk a look at him. "And now you have too much information." I shove my glasses back on, beyond embarrassed. I don't think I've ever told a man something so personal in my entire life. Even my doctor is a woman, so I can avoid these embarrassing conversations.

His hand slides under my hair, cupping the back of my neck before he kisses me just behind my ear, sending another zing through me. "Okay to no condom," he whispers in my ear before pulling back to look at me. "But we're going to wait until we get to the hotel. I want you in a bed."

I blink. We had all this conversation to work out the details, and then I have to wait? Unfair. "Why in a bed?"

"Why?" he growls before holding my face with both hands, kissing me and nipping my lower lip hard enough to shock me with the stinging pleasure. "Because." He releases me.

I stare at him, intrigued by the shift from chivalrous manners to commanding territory. I conclude that he's used to commanding because he's a prince. Regardless, I still want him, and I don't see why I have to wait just "because." Am I that resistible? Which brings me to another question.

"Lucas?"

His eyes are hooded, his voice gruff. "Yeah."

"Why didn't you join me last night? I mean, I was just across the living room."

His eyes smolder into mine, and my breath stalls. "Because I told myself I wasn't going to take advantage of your vulnerable state after what you'd been through." He scowls. "I already hate your ex, and I never met him."

A swell of emotions clogs my throat. "Oh," I manage. "That's sweet."

He leans his head back on the seat, closing his eyes and letting out a manly sigh. "Now that I know you're into it, it seems we're on the same page. A fun hookup, right?"

I nearly flinch but manage to say, "Right." That's all it is, a hookup, and I should be okay with that. He's making it clear this is nothing more than an itch that needs scratching. Simple, casual fun.

I fidget a bit, still achy and needy. Even after all this talk I didn't cool down enough to drop it. I don't want to wait anymore, and I'm just frustrated enough to say, "You got me really worked up in this limo and now you're making me wait. You know what I think? I think you're a-a tease."

His eyes flash, and I blurt, "Just kid—" which is as far as I get. He yanks me by the hips, landing me flat on my back, shoves my gown up past my waist, and pulls my lacey panties down and off.

My heart thunders in my chest, my breath coming harder. And then he shifts, lowering his head and dragging his tongue right down the center of me. I stop breathing.

"Jesus, you taste so good," he groans and dives back for more.

I'm lost in white-hot pleasure like I've never felt before. My brain shuts down, soft cries escaping my throat as he takes me up, higher and higher, and then I break hard, shuddering violently against him, my whole world going dim.

And when I come back to myself, there is nothing but Lucas's eyes gleaming at me with an intensity that tells me he's done teasing. My body hums, my pulse rushing through my veins. I've unleashed the wild beast. I just hope I can survive the ride with my heart intact.

Lucas

She threw herself at me. I would *not* have initiated. I told myself it had to be Alice who wanted it, her desire that made us cross the line no matter how badly I wanted her. Now I can't deny the urging of my body. Her sexy demands would've broken a less strong-willed man in that limo. She deserves better than a quick fuck in the backseat.

I can still taste her on my tongue. We're heading for the penthouse elevator at our hotel, and I'm dying to get to the room and inside her.

"Slow down," she says on a laugh as I pull her along with me.

I adjust my pace a bit, still holding her hand to make her hurry. The guards are following close behind us. Just Alice and I step into the private elevator, and the guards watch the doors close. They'll head to their room below us once they know we're heading up.

The moment the doors close, we slam together. I smack the button for our room, and then my hands slide all over her, my mouth hungry. I want her like I've never wanted another woman before. She's tugging my hair, her fingers fisted on the back of my shirt. Her moans only make me wilder to have her.

The doors open, and I tear myself away, grab her hand and race down the hall to the door. Then we're in, and I pull her straight to my bedroom, shut the door, and pin her against it, pressing my body fully against her softness, my mouth devouring hers. Need claws at me, and I struggle for restraint. I want her pleasure too.

I break the kiss and turn her, my breath labored as I unzip her gown. *Slow down.* I kiss her neck, and she leans back against me, tilting her head to the side to give me better access. She smells like flowers and sexy woman, and I don't know how much longer I can wait. I turn her to face me and slide the gown off her shoulders. It drops to her waist. I get only a brief glimpse of smooth creamy skin and full round breasts with rosy peaks that pebble into hard points under my gaze before she clutches the gown to her chest, covering up.

"Why don't we turn out the lights?" she asks brightly and turns them off.

Complete blackness.

I turn them back on. "I want to see you. What's wrong? I already saw you in the limo."

Her lashes flutter down. "That was under flattering dim light. Let me see if I can adjust..." She shifts the switch so dim I can barely see the outline of her.

"Do you always make love with the lights out?"

She giggles. "Make love."

I grunt, heat creeping up my neck. Here I am, trying to pull out the princely stops by not being crude, and she laughs. I slide the lights back on to maximum brightness. "Fuck," I growl, and she jolts. "Do you always *fuck* with the lights out?"

"Y-yes."

I gentle my voice as I lower the lights to half dim. "There." Then I decide we've talked enough. "Take off your dress *now*." And, because I'm a gentleman, I strip too.

~

Alice

Lucas strips in front of me. The reveal is so spectacular my grip slips from my dress and it drops to my hips. I forget about the light, forget about myself, forget everything. Blazer gone, bow tie and cummerbund gone, shirt gone.

I reach out with both hands, tracing the curves of his rounded shoulders. "Do you work out every day?"

He pulls my dress over my head and tosses it to the side. "First thing in the morning for an hour."

"Then how do you keep up the nightlife?"

He pulls me flush against him, his heat searing me. "I nap."

"You nap?" I echo in surprise.

"It's a power nap," he says defensively. "Very manly."

"So you get these results in just an hour?" I pull back to trace the lines and ridges along his torso, from pecs to abs to the deep V at his waist.

"You like?" he drawls before slowly unbuckling his belt, the button, the zipper. My mouth goes dry as his dress pants and boxer briefs slide down and then off.

I glimpse his thick cock, gulp, and look up to his glittering aquamarine eyes. He is the definition of male beauty, and I am in *awe*.

I slide my hands around his waist and feel my way along his back, exploring more fantastic lines and ridges.

He turns to give me a better view, winking at me over his shoulder.

I guess I am ogling. "Well worth your efforts." I can't stop gazing at the spectacular view. "You're so beautiful I almost want to take a picture to gaze at later." I look up at him in question just in case that might be a go.

"So you can masturbate to it? Nope. You're doing all your coming with me."

His hand cups the back of my neck, his fingers tangling in my hair. My breath hitches. He gives my hair a tug, tipping my face up to his. "Enough looking," he says before his mouth claims mine. And it is a claiming, a wild kiss full of need and raw hunger. I can do nothing but cling to him, overwhelmed by the kind of passion I've only dreamed about. His other hand slides to my ass, pressing me against him, making me ache. The world falls away. There is nothing but his taste, his scent, his hard body pressed against me.

My hands are all over him, my mouth just as hungry as I press close, needing closer, needing him inside me.

I tear my mouth away and kick off my pumps. "I want you so much."

He makes short work of my bra and panties, and I wait impatiently for him to kiss me breathless again.

His eyes go dark, heated, as he takes in my naked body with open appreciation. He cups my jaw and kisses me. "So fucking sexy, Alice."

"Ohhh," I say on a soft sigh. "You too."

He bends a little, and I think he's about to kiss my breast, my nipples tightening in anticipation, but then he shocks me. I yelp as he scoops me off the ground, cradled in his arms, and carries me to the bed.

"Lucas! What are you doing?"

"Being romantic."

"I don't want you to hurt your back."

He scoffs, all manly pride. "Why do I work out if not to carry a sexy woman to my bed?"

"Because you like women panting after you."

He grins and gently sets me on the mattress. "I like you panting after me. I like carrying you to my bed."

I can't help my smile. Somehow he knew I needed that little adjustment from "a sexy woman" to the more specific "you."

He joins me, brushing my hair back from my face and kissing me tenderly. "That sweet smile of yours gets me every time."

I'm surprised once again, but before I can come up with an appropriate response, he's kissing me, nudging my legs apart, and settling between them. His weight is so welcome, the heat of him so satisfying. My hands roam the hard planes of his back down to his ass, pulling him closer. He takes the hint, breaking our kiss to guide himself inside me.

He groans, tipping his head back as he reaches full hilt. It makes me even hotter to see his obvious pleasure.

I gasp as he thrusts deep. He slowly withdraws and I tip my hips up, eager for more. His pace is hard and fast and so-o-o-o good. I can't help my moans, and then he angles himself just right, triggering something powerful inside me. Fuck. This must be the G-spot I've heard about. It's…omigod.

"Lucas!" I cry out.

His mouth covers mine, his tongue invading, his thrusts just right. I stiffen, and then I explode, my harsh cry swallowed by his mouth. He lifts his head, watching me as he thrusts over and over, bringing wave after wave of pleasure. I thrash my head from side to side, drowning in sensation. It's too much, too intense. "Lucas, I'm done!"

"We're not done. Open your eyes, Alice."

I do, my breath quickening at his heated gaze. He pumps into me, slower now, drawing it out. I tremble under him, overwhelmed, my breathing ragged. He thrusts hard, making me gasp as he leans close to my ear. "Your turn." He pulls out, rolling to his back, and pulling me with him.

I try to catch my breath, still shaky as Lucas arranges me over him, lifting me by the hips and slowly impaling me onto him. I moan, gripping his shoulders, nearly at the brink again. I don't think I ever left it. I instinctively move, setting a fast pace that has me racing to release.

Lucas grabs my hips, stilling me, and I mewl in protest. I want, I want…ohh. He shifts me, pushing me more upright, his hands on my breasts, caressing and squeezing. I move again, experimentally, trying out this new feeling. Everything feels so good. I glance down at his face. His eyes are closed, his jaw tight almost like he's in pain.

I still. "Am I hurting you?"

His eyes fly open; the intensity in them enthralls me. "No. I fucking love it." His hand slides to my ass, cupping it as he urges me on with a firm hand.

I take the hint, rocking my hips as he keeps me in his grip. And then I let go, taking him deep over and over. His gaze is locked on mine and then both his hands cup my breasts, his fingers closing in, pinching my nipples. My eyes roll back in my head at the intense pleasure. I buck wildly, out of control, dimly aware of his deep voice urging me on. The orgasm slams into me along with his hissed, "Yesss."

I rock mindlessly and then I still, spent. Lucas grips my hips, guiding my movements to take more and more. Soft whimpers escape my throat, caught in the endless rush of pleasure, and then he surges deep, setting me off again. He goes off this time too, his head arched back, the cords of his neck prominent as he groans his pleasure. My lips curve at the beautiful sight. I arch my hips again, wanting to give him more pleasure, but he clamps his hands on my hips and stills me.

"I'm done," he says on a groan.

I lean down and kiss him. "How come when I say I'm

done, you say we're not done. But when you're done, then it's game over."

He smiles. "Because you're the multi-orgasmic one."

I kiss his neck, giving him a nip. "I am now."

He groans and then he laughs. "I'm going to have so much fun with you."

14

Lucas

A short while later, I tuck Alice against my side and arrange the covers over us. I don't usually like to spend the night with my hookups, but this is not a casual hookup. I let her think it was light and casual to ease her in. I want more, and I know she's not ready yet.

She traces a circle over my chest. "That was a first."

"First time with a sex god like me?"

Her head pops up to look at me. "That too. It was a lot of firsts."

I stare at her. *A lot?* "Which part?"

She settles her head back on my chest. "First time with the lights on, first time I wasn't on the bottom, first time finding my G-spot, first time I climaxed during sex, first time I was multi-orgasmic." She gives me a squeeze around the middle. "You're amazing!"

I still. I'm not sure where to begin with that. Yes, it's a compliment, but it's also a sad state of affairs for a woman as passionate as Alice.

She goes on, filling in the blanks. "I always thought keeping the light off was more flattering for everyone, you know? But I *loved* seeing you in all your manly glory."

A wide smile spreads across my face. "Thanks."

"And you made me feel beautiful," she whispers.

My arm tightens around her. I hate that anyone made her feel less than. "That's because you are."

She kisses my chest. "Thanks. And I actually liked being on top. Usually I'm on the bottom."

"By your choice?"

"Well, yeah, then I don't have to worry about crushing you with my weight or that my boobs bounce too much."

I pause at this, part surprised that she thinks she could actually crush me and part aroused thinking of her bouncing boobs. They're magnificent. She's magnificent.

"It was nice of you to hold my bouncing boobs," she adds.

I bite back a laugh. "Yes, well, I aim to please." I focus back on her sad lack of orgasms. "You never climaxed during sex before? How could you stand being left unsatisfied?"

"I was ultimately satisfied. You know, after."

"After sex?"

"After he fell asleep."

I burst out laughing. I can't help it.

She glares at me. "What's so funny?"

I try to contain myself. "Nothing. At least I know you like sex. You just haven't had the right lover before."

She huffs before admitting, "You're right, and I deserve great sex. I'm a healthy woman with a decent libido and an indecent imagination."

I kiss her. "Now that I can work with."

"Totally," she says on a sigh. "Did I crush you when I was on top? I'm not a lightweight." Her gaze shifts to the side. "Understatement."

I cup her jaw and turn her back to me. I want her to see the truth in my eyes. "You could never crush me. I'm six feet of solid muscle, and you're a tiny thing."

Her brow wrinkles, vulnerability lurking in her eyes. "I'm not tiny. Five feet five is average, but I'm also what you call a curvy girl. Surely you noticed. They didn't even have my size at the shop."

I run my hand down the slope of her back and over her curvy ass, giving her a squeeze. "I don't care what size dress you wear, and I've been lusting after your lush curves since the first time I saw you. I know I'm a pig. You can hate on me for that, just let me enjoy you."

She smiles that smile that wraps around my heart. "You're a sweet pig. And you sound sincere, but I've seen pictures of you with many twiggy women with giant fake boobs, no hips, and long pencil stick legs."

"I want *you*, Alice. I need you more than I've ever needed anyone before."

She goes very still, and I tense, afraid I've screwed up, needing her so much.

"You mean," she says slowly, "that maybe you didn't know what you were missing with those other women?"

"Yes." She said it so much better than I could.

She hugs me, plastering herself against me. Heat radiates through my chest along with a bone-deep sense of satisfaction. She has real affection for me, and it's a fantastic start.

I stroke her soft hair. "While we're discussing all things sexy, here's something to improve your male point-of-view scenes, men are visual creatures. For the man, it's about seeing and then feeling sexy curves, and primal urgency. That's it. No man spouts poetry in the heat of passion."

"But it's so much more romantic that way," she pouts.

I nip her lower lip. "Not one man on the planet would ever. He shouldn't even be able to think of any word beyond *fuck* and *more*, not if he's passionate about a woman."

She strokes my beard, looking thoughtful. "Next time will you narrate your experience of sex from your manly point of view?"

"No."

I kiss her and then I can't resist kissing her again, longer this time. I roll on top of her, nuzzling into her neck, breathing in her sexy flowery scent, needing her once again.

～

It's Monday morning, and I'm heading for my official meeting at the bank with Jules. It's the first time I've left Alice's side since we arrived, and the strange thing is how much I resent having to leave her back at the hotel. She's fine, happy even, because when I'm not introducing her to the pleasures previously only enjoyed in her imagination—and she has a fantastic erotic imagination—she's been in a frenzy of writing. I'm trying to take it as a compliment that I'm endlessly inspiring, but I fear what I really am is a distraction from her main obsession, her book, whereas she is my main obsession. Hell. This was supposed to be a temporary arrangement for a specific purpose, which is almost finished, and I don't want it to end. Not that I want to actually be engaged. I just want to enjoy her longer, see how it plays out. That might not even be an option because Alice is already talking about getting back to Villroy, finishing her overdue manuscript, and personally delivering it to her editor in New York City in her "glorious moment of triumph." She's mentioned her future triumphant return twice. Not once has she mentioned me in that future.

Maybe all I am is inspiration.

Maybe this is karma slapping me in the face for being so cavalier about the women in my life.

Maybe I'm in love.

I halt right there on the sidewalk. Is that what this is? This agitated state where nothing feels right unless she's in my arms? This is *horrible*. If that's what this is, then I hate love, especially because I know she doesn't love me back. If she did, she wouldn't be so eager to get back to work and back to the US. She'd be finding ways to prolong our time together. How did I let myself fall for the one woman who has no interest in falling? Why did I pick someone so emotionally unavailable? I knew she was a mess coming off a botched engagement. It's like I purposely sabotaged myself. Maybe I really do have a fear of commitment and this just proves it. I can only love someone who can't love me back.

I scrub a hand over my face. Maybe I should tell her how I

feel. Maybe it's not just me. I turn and see the matching stone-faced expressions of my guards, Louis and Michael. They're probably wondering why I'm just standing here on the sidewalk instead of going to my meeting. "I'm thinking," I say, though neither of them voiced the question.

Louis inclines his head slightly. Michael remains impassive.

I turn back around and stride toward the bank. I'm here to do one job—secure a loan for Villroy. I'm the goddamn CFO. I can't let myself get all caught up in the messy emotional swamp of a relationship I was trying to avoid in the first place.

It's your own fault for seducing her.

No, she seduced me.

You crossed the line, and you know it. You have no one to blame but yourself.

I'm going insane, arguing with myself. I open the door to the bank and step inside, heading straight to the receptionist to let Jules know I'm here.

A few minutes later, I'm shown into his office and another man, David, joins us. David looks to be in his fifties with thinning brown hair and what may be a permanent frown, the lines etched deep into his face. He's in charge of construction loans. Jules works on business loans, and I was not aware they were separate departments. It seems I'm not quite as close to the finish line as I'd thought. We need a construction loan to expand the manufacturing facilities, though it wouldn't hurt to have extra capital to staff up as well.

After brief pleasantries, I hand over my proposal and go over the numbers, hoping they'll see that our plan for Villroy's new business venture is a relatively sure thing. We've already got an established fishing industry. We're just taking what we have and shifting it into another product. The fishermen will still be involved, even still fishing, though for a different kind of catch. Local ingredients from the sea, including fish oil, sponges, and sea salt, will go into the manufacturing of a cosmetics line, which will be featured and sold at the day spa. We might even expand to selling the cosmetics on the larger global market. Plus there's room for more construction on the flat plot of land by the spa, maybe an upscale seafood restaurant.

"Everything seems to be in order," Jules says. "I think you've made a good case here." He turns to David. "What do you think?"

David frowns and folds his hands on top of the round bulge of his stomach. "Jules, I know you have a friendship with the king of Villroy, which makes you partial to their cause, but I would like more information. I'd like to see what they're doing over there."

I jump in. "Of course, you're welcome any time. A site visit is no problem. You'll see the spa is nearly complete, and I can show you where we hope to expand the manufacturing."

Jules and David have a quick chat about possible meeting times before landing on Wednesday.

"Wednesday is great," I say, standing to shake their hands. They both stand to return the gesture. "Thank you for your confidence. I'm sure you'll feel even better after visiting."

"I'm sure we will," Jules says with a smile. "How is your fiancée? Celeste was quite taken with her. Said she was a delight."

My chest puffs out with pride. I chose well. Wait, I didn't choose her. Anna set this whole thing up. I'm the only one who fell. That dampens my enthusiasm, tempering my voice. "She is a delight, thank you."

"Will she be at the site visit?" Jules asks.

"I could ask her to join us."

"Wonderful. I look forward to it."

David nods at me and takes his leave.

I head out the door, eager to get back to Alice to tell her the good news from the bank. Then I realize I should be reporting back to Gabriel and Anna first. I call Gabriel and get his voicemail.

"It's Lucas. Looks like it's a go for the bank loan. Jules came through for us. He just wants to do a site visit with another banker and then we should be good. On my way home."

The moment I get back to the suite, I go to Alice's bedroom. She's set up with her laptop on a small desk facing the window, her noise-cancelling headphones on. I don't want to startle her. Her fingers aren't moving, which means she's thinking. I slip into her peripheral vision and wait for her to notice me.

"Oh, you're back already!" She takes the headphones off and sets them on the desk, clicking save on her document. She's OCD about saving. "Is that bad or good?"

I can't help but touch her. I smooth a lock of her soft blond hair behind her ear, lean down and kiss her. "It's good. They're doing a site visit on Villroy on Wednesday to check everything out, and then we should be a go."

She leaps up and throws her arms around me. "That's wonderful! I'm so happy for you!"

I breathe her in, the scent of flowers and Alice. "You were a big part of it. They could tell I was serious and more of a committed man than a globe-trotting man."

She draws back, giving me her sweet smile. My heart thumps harder. "It's easy to play fiancée with you. If you'd been my real fiancé before, I probably wouldn't have gotten writer's block. It wasn't that I was so busy planning the wedding, I mean, I was, but it was also that I wasn't being true to myself. I realized I was twisting myself to be who he expected and wanted. Like he loved cycling, so I went cycling, even though I hated it and it hurt my crotch." I stifle a laugh; sometimes her turn of phrase is just funny. "Or the fact that I went on a crash diet after he proposed because he said I needed to look good in our wedding pictures."

Fury spikes through me. "That ass! He insulted you, made you deprive yourself, all while he was cheating on you!" I swear if I ever meet her ex, I'm going to punch him right in the mouth.

She flushes pink. "It's nice that you take my side."

"Anyone would. He was a total prick and you deserve much better."

Her gaze searches mine. "Would you still have wanted me if I was twenty-four pounds heavier? This is me after the diet. I was even heavier in high school."

My gut tightens, angry at every person who ever made her feel bad about herself. "Well, you're not in high school," I say lightly, brushing my thumb over her cheek. "And that was an oddly specific number."

She glances down at herself, smoothing a hand over her soft stomach.

I grab her hand and kiss her palm. "Yes, I would have wanted you no matter what because you're sexy as fuck, and you'd have more curves."

She looks skeptical. "More of me to love, huh?"

My mouth goes dry. Should I say something about the love thing? This could be the opening I need. I could say, "No, not more of you, just you. I think I love you, Alice." But do I think it, or do I know it? How do you know for sure?

"You don't have to answer that," she says quietly. "Men are visual creatures. You explained that."

My hesitation made her fill in the blank with the wrong thing. She does that sometimes, not yet confident in her appeal. Who could blame her with the way her ex treated her?

I keep it light. "Would you still want me if I was twenty-four percent bald?" I pull back my hair from my forehead, covering it with both hands. No worries for me, this thick hair is here to stay.

She laughs, and I smile. "Bald is sexy." She kisses me, her fingers grazing my beard. "How much time do we have before we have to go back to Villroy?"

"As long as you want," I reply in a husky voice, already thinking of the naked possibilities.

"Great!" Then she sits down at the desk, puts her headphones on, and starts typing.

I stand there, passed over again for her book, and watch the words form on the page. The scoundrel is at it again. She called me a scoundrel before. Am I the hero of her story?

She glances over her shoulder at me, lifting the headphones off one ear. "Don't watch, okay?"

"I guess it's a compliment that you can write around me since your ex gave you writer's block." *Not an insult that you keep going back to your story because I'm so forgettable,* I add silently.

She gives me her sweet smile, and my chest tightens. I need that smile in my life. "It means all is right in my world."

I can't help my wide smile. I did that. I made everything right in her world, and somehow she did the same for me. Now I just have to figure out how to make this a real relationship.

~

Alice

We get back to Villroy in time for dinner with Lucas's family in the formal dining room. He wanted everyone to be there to share the good news about the bankers. I'm a little nervous to meet Gabriel, the king, not to mention meeting his other brothers, Prince Oscar and Prince Adrian. That's a lot of royalty all in one room. At least I feel comfortable with Anna. She's an Alice fangirl. Ha-ha!

Lucas has been quite the chivalrous guy, even when we're in private. I guess all that sex made him want to do nice things for me. I want to do nice things for him too. He's made me feel so good and, after being at such a low point in my life, I can't help but feel affectionate toward him. I don't have any relationship expectations. I know who he is, and the truth is, I'm not ready for a relationship. That doesn't mean I won't enjoy him while I can.

We're in the hallway just outside the dining room when my phone rings, startling me. Crap. I forgot to put it on vibrate. That could've been a big royal faux pas. I fish it out of my purse and see a voicemail alert from Mason. There's four texts too. I quickly tap over in case it's my editor or my parents, but they're all urgent-sounding texts from Mason.

Where are you? Please call me back.

We really need to talk.

Alice, it's important. Call me.

At least text me. Where are you?

I turn the phone to vibrate and put it back in my purse.

Lucas lets out a breath that brushes my ear. "He doesn't deserve your attention."

I glance up at him. "I know. I think he's at the groveling stage. The more texts and voicemails I get, the more apologies I imagine piling up. And then, when they ultimately stop, I'll know he's given up in wretched desolation. It's my own quiet revenge."

One corner of his mouth lifts. "As long as it's for villainous reasons."

Once we're in the dining room, Lucas rests his hand on my lower back as he guides me to my seat. We dressed for dinner, Lucas in a navy blue suit, no tie, and me in a wine red short-sleeved dress with a skirt that swings up in a round flare if I do a spin, which, of course, I had to do several of in my room. Two men who must be his brothers are already seated across the table in button-down shirts, no blazers, joking around with each other. I'm betting Lucas dressed up more because of his need to impress Gabriel with his business triumph. He wants to be seen as CEO material. I must say, looking at his brothers in real life for the first time, the resemblance is strong in this family (apologies to Mr. Skywalker). Same thick dark brown hair, same angular cheekbones, full sensual lips, and wide shoulders. In my completely unbiased opinion, though, Lucas is the best-looking one.

"Hello," Lucas says to his brothers, "glad you're both here. This is Alice."

They stand to greet me as Lucas says, "My brothers, Oscar and Adrian."

"I'm Oscar," one of the men says, walking around the table and offering his hand.

Up close, he's so stunning I flush hot from head to toe. *Sorry, Lucas.* I don't know what it is about Oscar. His eyes match Lucas's blue-green eyes. He has sexy scruff, but otherwise is similar to Lucas, just a teensy bit different. I belatedly thrust out my hand and he lifts it, dropping a kiss on the back of it, his gaze warm on mine. Like he knows the effect he has on women.

"Enough," Lucas snaps.

A small smile plays over Oscar's lips as he murmurs to me, "You're lovely." He releases my hand and then picks it up again, examining my ring. "This ring is exquisite." He turns to Lucas. "Isn't this Grandmother's ring?"

I laugh, pulling my hand from his and admiring the ring. "Oh no! It looks like the real thing, but it was actually a bargain from an online jewelry store because of its flaws."

Oscar and Lucas exchange a look.

Wait, what? *Is* it a precious family heirloom? Oh my God. I wore this ring when I wrapped my hand around Lucas's cock and when I gripped his ass! Granted, it was a royal ruby pressed against a royal cock and a royal ass, but still. *Stop thinking about cock and ass!* I flush hot. I even showered with this ring, soap and shampoo running willy-nilly over a flawless ruby and diamonds. This thing should be in a maximum-security vault under pure-air, no-light conditions, or whatever they do for precious jewels. And to think every time I marveled over how beautiful it looked, Lucas never reacted. Why did he tell me it was a bargain online?

"She's my fiancée," Lucas bites out. "She needed an engagement ring."

"Oh!" I exclaim. "We played a little fake-engagement game. I helped him look grounded for business matters, and he gave me inspiration for my story. I'm a romance author, and fake engagements are very popular with readers."

Oscar stares at Lucas. "You're fake engaged?"

"Yes. And don't say a word in front of Gabriel."

I stare at Lucas. "Why?"

Lucas shakes his head. "Later."

Something's not right here.

Oscar's brows lift. "Oh-kay." He turns to me. "Are you Anna's friend?"

I open my mouth to answer when Lucas says belligerently, like Oscar's curiosity is a personal affront, "Yes. We met through Anna." Maybe Lucas is being protective, making sure I don't have to explain my solo honeymoon. I suppose it was my American accent that made Oscar think that. I'd like to be Anna's friend, anyway.

Oscar's eyes sparkle with good humor. "Congratulations on your fake engagement."

Adrian joins us, glancing at the ring before meeting my eyes in an assessing way. His eyes are hazel, unlike his brothers', and he has heavy scruff like he forgot to shave. Or maybe he's growing a beard. "Very nice to meet you, Alice."

"Thank you," I say. "Nice to meet you too."

Adrian and Oscar head back to their seats. Lucas's hand returns to my lower back, guiding me to my chair, which he pulls out for me, sliding it back in as I take my seat. "Thank you," I murmur.

"My pleasure," he says and takes the seat next to mine.

Oscar makes a big deal out of pulling out Adrian's chair for him.

"Shut it," Lucas snaps.

"Did I say something?" Oscar chuckles and takes his seat, saying to Adrian, "Looks like Lucas did learn something during those mandatory etiquette lessons."

"Just took the right motivation," Adrian says with a smile.

"Ignore them, please," Lucas tells me.

"How long have you two been together?" Oscar asks.

"Are you together?" Adrian asks.

"Obviously they are," Oscar says. "Look at how he looks at her. And have you ever seen him actually use any of that etiquette shoved down our throats?"

"She looks uncomfortable," Adrian observes. "Maybe it's just a game."

"With our grandmother's ring?" Oscar asks incredulously.

I fidget in my seat. We're not together. Or are we? I'm confused. Are we friends with spectacular benefits, or something more?

Lucas's hand closes over mine under the table, giving it a squeeze. "We're together."

I turn to him, nerves racing through me, unsure what it means.

He cups the back of my neck, drawing me close and whispering directly in my ear, "You're mine, and I don't want them to get any ideas."

I shiver at the raw possession in his voice. When did this happen? Did I somehow fall into a committed relationship? I break out into a cold sweat. I'm not ready for this.

And how crazy is it that Lucas thinks his gorgeous brothers would also be interested in me? Me, the same woman who's only had a handful of lukewarm offers from men in all of my twenty-three years would suddenly have three gorgeous princes fighting over me? The writer in me considers the possibilities for my next book. Everything is fodder for my next book. At least now I have more interesting things to write about than a love triangle with crushed men.

"Alice?"

I snap to attention, glancing at Oscar and Adrian, unsure which one spoke. "Yes?"

"Since you're involved with my brother," Oscar says with a devilish smile, "you should know that Lucas once ran naked from the waist down straight into our mother, the *queen*'s garden party."

I grin, my mind playing out the scene. A proper garden party among royalty. A naked Lucas. Wait. "How old were you?" I ask Lucas.

"I was seven," he says drily.

"While the queen of Alvilda was visiting," Oscar adds, his eyes dancing with amusement.

I giggle, filling in a seven-year-old naked Lucas dashing through, flashing everyone. The proper queens, teacups stalling halfway to their lips.

"I was running from the doctor's needle," Lucas says in his defense.

"I was five and waiting my dignified turn," Oscar shoots back.

Lucas jabs a finger at Oscar. "He couldn't say his Rs when he was little. Every time he asked for a fork, the whole family thought he was asking for a fuck."

"What the fork, Oscar?" Adrian quips.

"Where my fuck?" Oscar says in an innocent boyish voice. "I need my fuck."

We all crack up. The brothers keep up their banter, ratting each other out to me with their hilarious histories. They did run wild around here. I'm laughing so much I forget to worry over the whole relationship thing. Servants arrive, presenting us with drinks, and quietly leave us to our conversation.

I'm enjoying my wine, feeling surprisingly relaxed with the royal company when a servant enters and intones, "Their Majesties, King Gabriel and Queen Anna."

I straighten up, thinking I should stand and curtsy, but everyone else remains seated, so I just bow my head to them. Gabriel is dressed formally in a charcoal suit with tie, his jaw clenched tight, his expression grim as he walks Anna toward the head of the table, his hand on the small of her back.

"Hello, everyone," Anna says, positively glowing. She's dressed stylishly in a pale pink short-sleeved dress with a deep V in front and a cute bow on the side. She's rocking the pregnancy look.

A chorus of hellos follow. She squeezes my shoulder as she passes me. "Good to see you again, Alice."

I smile, turning to see her. "You too." She stops short, staring at my hand tucked in Lucas's hand, where it rests on top of his thigh. That's where he put it. I pull my hand free and the ruby ring catches the light, glittering. I quickly tuck my hand under my leg.

Anna meets my eyes with a pleased look. She was, after all, the one who came up with the fake-engagement plan.

"You're glowing with your pregnancy," I say.

She rubs a hand over her large rounded belly, smiling down at it. "Thank you."

"Gabriel, this is Alice," Lucas says.

I turn to a glowering Gabriel towering over me, and swallow hard. I bow my head, a little shaken by Gabriel's glower. "Nice to meet you, Your Majesty."

"You too, Alice," he says formally.

Something is going on with him, and I fear I'm about to witness a showdown between him and Lucas, who, as far as I know, is the one with the biggest beef with him. I look to Lucas, but his expression is impassive.

Gabriel is seated at the head of the table now, Anna next to him. The brothers are all serious and quiet. Is Gabriel a party killer? There's a definite tension in the air. Gabriel signals for a servant, and a man rushes forward to pour water for Anna and then for him. I suspect Gabriel has ordered it this way in deference to his wife's pregnancy. Surely, warm, friendly Anna wouldn't have chosen to marry Gabriel if he was always glowering and intimidating, right?

Only a few moments later, two servants file into the room with platters of the first course, a cold soup.

"Hope you like gazpacho," Anna says. "I had a craving."

"Whatever the baby wants," Oscar says.

Anna grins. "Careful, sometimes she wants macaroni and cheese with ketchup."

The brothers groan in disgust. Gabriel remains silent, his gaze on me and then Lucas. He does not look happy.

I focus on my soup. I'm thinking maybe Lucas should tell Gabriel his good banker news to ratchet down the tension level in here, but I keep quiet in case Lucas is waiting for a special moment.

The table is silent as we enjoy our soup, the only sound

the occasional clink of a spoon. Then Gabriel says sharply, "I heard from Jules."

Lucas straightens, setting his spoon down. "Yes. It's looking good. I was going to share the good news after we ate. I believe I can sign off on the loan after the site visit on Wednesday. They just want to see what we're doing here."

"That's wonderful!" Anna exclaims.

"Nice work," Oscar says. Adrian smiles and keeps eating.

Gabriel remains serious. "Lucas, you went behind my back with your ridiculous engagement idea after I specifically told you not to. Jules mentioned it, catching me off guard."

I suck in air. I didn't know the king was opposed to the idea. Why didn't Lucas tell me? I never would've gone through with it if I knew the king was against it.

Lucas lied to me.

My gut knots, bile rising in my throat. It was a lie of omission, but still a lie. After he swore on his life to always be one hundred percent honest with me. He said he was a man of honor, and I believed him. After everything I've been through, he knows how important honesty is to me. I trusted him.

Lucas is not the man I thought he was. I need a man of integrity. Not someone who deceives because it's convenient to do so. I can't be with someone like that, especially after Mason and Riley's feast of lies. I desperately want to bolt, but I feel too shaky to manage it.

"Everything worked out fine," Lucas says dismissively.

I tense. Even being a newcomer, I know his casual tone is going to irk the king. What happens if you go against the wishes of the king? My mind whirls with the hideous possibilities—excommunication, exile, moldering away in a dungeon for life.

Anna pipes up. "I agree with Lucas. Everything worked out."

I'm frozen in place, sick to my stomach, unsure what to do or say.

Gabriel turns to Anna. "Did you know that Lucas went forward with the engagement after I told him not to?"

"No," she says solemnly. She turns to look at me and Lucas, and then back to her husband. "But I hoped."

"You hoped?" he echoes in a quiet voice that's somehow more intimidating than a shout.

"Yes!" she exclaims, gesturing toward us. "It's romantic! And Alice needed the inspiration for her story."

Gabriel scowls. "Oh, well, if Alice needs inspiration, by all means—"

"Enough," Lucas barks, drawing everyone's attention. "Leave Alice out of it."

"I will," Gabriel bites out. "I blame you entirely, and when this blows up in your face, which it will, I want nothing to do with it, and you will have no further role in our business."

My stomach drops. Lucas went forward with our fake engagement even knowing he could be cut out of the business that means so much to him? Why would he do that? The only reason I can think of is that he does whatever it takes to reach his goal by any means necessary. I don't believe the ends always justify the means. Honor and integrity are important.

"Gabriel," Anna says softly, and then whispers something to him.

He cups her jaw, brushing his thumb across her cheek in a tender gesture. "Darling, you're exempt from blame due to the advanced state of your pregnancy making you sentimental."

"Not everything is hormones!" she protests.

Servants enter, and the room goes quiet again as drinks are refreshed. I quickly drain my wine and accept another.

Lucas speaks up as soon as the servants leave. "Conservative bankers value the institution of marriage. We need to keep it going."

My throat tightens, my eyes hot. Why does it hurt so much to know he's using me to fix his image? We're using each other.

I let him get too close is the problem. Otherwise, why would I be so upset over him?

"The truth will get out," Gabriel says, "which is why I was against it in the first place."

"People believe us," Lucas says. "No one would question it."

"And why are you so damned confident?" Gabriel asks.

"Because she's mine," Lucas says in a firm voice that brooks no argument.

The room goes utterly silent. Everyone is staring at Lucas, including me.

I grip my napkin tightly in my lap as I speak up loud and clear. "Lucas, I am not yours."

His jaw clenches, but he says nothing.

I turn to Gabriel, the words tumbling out in a rush. "I only wanted to help, Your Majesty. I won't go to the site visit with the bankers. I'm very sorry. I didn't know you were opposed to the fake-engagement idea, and I confess that I went along with it in no small part to help my story because I've had serious writer's block and the book is so overdue. If Jules asks, you can just say the engagement ended under mutual agreement."

Gabriel inclines his head regally. "Alice, thank you. It would be wise to end the charade as you said. If only Lucas had some of your good sense. I don't blame you. From what I understand, you were in an unusually vulnerable state. I'm sorry my errant brother took advantage."

I glance at Lucas, who's scowling, and turn back to Gabriel, my heart in my throat. "No advantage taken." I'm the one who threw myself at him in that limo, stupidly thinking our solid friendship would make casual sex possible. Except I'm hurting too much right now for it to truly have been casual. I'm such a mess. I wanted casual, terrified of a relationship, only now I realize it is a relationship of sorts, and it has to end. He broke my trust, broke his word.

"Vulnerable state?" Oscar asks, looking around the table. "Would somebody please fill me in?"

Anna shakes him off, glancing at Gabriel meaningfully.

"You can't back out," Lucas says, turning to me. "Jules likes you. He likes who I am with you."

I blink rapidly, fighting back tears. I need to step away to protect my vulnerable heart. It's barely pieced together as it is.

"You mean the princely manners?" Oscar asks. He turns to Anna. "He even pulled out her chair for her."

"I'm curious too," Anna says. "Who are you with her?"

Lucas turns to Anna. "I'm me, only more grounded. Respectable."

I can't take any more. I stand and glance around the table. "Excuse me, everyone. I'm not very hungry after all." I push back my chair, and Lucas grabs my wrist. "Let go," I snap.

"I'll go with you."

I lean down and whisper, "No. I need to be alone right now." He releases me, and I tell everyone goodnight. I'm barely out the door when I hear Anna's loud exclamation.

"Dammit! You scared her away!"

I shake my head and keep going. I'm not scared. I'm being smart. The red flag with Lucas is impossible to ignore —he lied. Game over.

15

———

Lucas

I give Alice some time to cool down before going up to her suite in the east wing. I imagine she's typing furiously at her laptop with her headphones on, blocking out the world the way she does. She's upset that I went against Gabriel's wishes, but I knew it would be fine. And some part of me knew the attraction was too strong to keep away from her. I wanted to play her fiancé and make her smile by pulling out all the princely stops she dreamed of. All I have to do is explain it to her. She's a romantic sort and will enjoy hearing my romantic-sounding intentions.

I knock just in case she can hear it, but she doesn't answer. I push open the door and find her sitting on the living room sofa with her laptop, headphones on, her fingers fast and furious. She's probably making sure the scoundrel (me) gets his comeuppance. I need to read this story. If people make the connection between me and the scoundrel in her story, and the fact that Alice and I are together, it'll only damage my family's reputation further. My rep is already on shaky ground. It could get ugly, especially if someone discovers we lied about the engagement.

I step into her peripheral vision, and she startles, taking her headphones off. She frowns. "You should've knocked."

"I did." I sit next to her on the sofa. "I'd love to read your story."

Her lips form a mutinous line. "You'll have to wait until it's published. On second thought, no, you can't read it. Oh, wait. You don't care about no. You just do whatever you want —" her fingers dance through the air "—and think that charm and your crooked smile will let you get away with anything." She hits save, closes the laptop with a bang, and sets it on the coffee table. "Excuse me. I'm very tired."

"Alice."

She stares straight ahead. "What?"

"I'm sorry you got caught up in Gabriel's anger."

Her eyes flash. "Don't apologize for your brother. This isn't about him. You disobeyed your king and conveniently kept it from me, which dragged me into the fray."

"That's what I was trying to say. I don't want you in the fray."

She looks up at me, hurt in her eyes. "Why didn't you tell me he was against it? I never would've gone through with it. You deliberately kept this from me." Her voice chokes. "A lie of omission is still a lie. You swore on your life to be honest with me."

I take her hand, and she yanks it away. I blow out a breath. "I went through with it because I liked being your dream fiancé. You deserve that."

Her eyes well. "You could've told me. You know how much I need honesty after what I've been through."

I speak from the heart. "I didn't tell you because I didn't think you'd go through with it, and I wanted to be with you. Making it a game was the easiest way to get closer to you."

She shakes her head and swipes at a tear. "Stop acting charming. You went through with it to cement your business deal. You used me."

I gesture toward her laptop. "And you used me too. We both understood that going in, but that's not what it is now."

"I need to be smart this time," she whispers. "You got what you wanted; I got what I wanted. So now…"

"What?"

She shakes her head, staring at the floor. "I guess I'm done playing the game."

I dip my head, trying to catch her gaze. "It's not a game anymore. You must know that."

She lifts her chin, but it wobbles. My chest constricts at her obvious distress. Her voice is wobbly too. "I was only using you for my story, so be careful how you treat me from here on out because it's all going in there." She jabs her finger toward her laptop, staring at it, away from me.

"That would be an honor. And I will treat you well."

"You did not act honorably," she says through her teeth. "I no longer trust you."

"I had good romantic intentions."

"I think they were mixed intentions at best. And you're not even a romantic. That's me."

"Alice, if I had a chance to do it all over again, I still wouldn't tell you that Gabriel was against the engagement because then I would've missed out on getting to know you. I would've missed discovering sweet, gentle Alice with a resilient strength all wrapped around a tender vulnerability. And that is the one hundred percent truth. Please don't shut me out because I wanted to be with you."

She looks up at me, her gaze searching mine, maybe to see if I mean it. I do. She sighs. "Lucas, I don't think—"

"You're mine." It comes out harsh because for the first time I fear I'm losing her.

"I'm not yours," she grinds out. "I'm my own woman."

I tuck a lock of hair behind her ear and lower my voice. "Yes, you are your own woman." I graze the side of her neck with my fingertips, and her eyes go half-mast. She enjoys my touch as much as I enjoy hers. I shift my hand, holding her jaw, my voice low and firm, my eyes intent on hers. "And you're still mine."

She exhales sharply, her eyes flashing. "I can't do this with you! You think you can just keep messing with people for your own purposes!" She deflates and says quietly, "I don't want to fight with you."

If this is fighting with Alice, I don't mind it. Everything she says, everything she does just draws me in. And I can't help but think she has some real feeling for me. Otherwise, she wouldn't be so hurt over what she thinks is a betrayal of her trust. She's skittish because of her recent breakup. I'll show her otherwise. I would never betray her.

"I don't want to fight either, sweet Alice."

She blinks a few times, seemingly thrown by the term of endearment.

I press my advantage, pinching her chin as I lean in and place a soft kiss on the corner of her mouth. Her sigh brushes over my lips. I kiss the other corner and she shifts, seeking more. I pull back, gazing into her soft blue eyes. "I want to be with you, Alice, no matter what we call it. Don't shut me out." I wrap her hair around my fist and tug, exposing her throat. She swallows visibly. I slowly lean in, dropping a kiss on the sensitive spot behind her ear, nuzzling the side of her neck, kissing and tasting my way down her throat.

I lift my head, our lips a breath apart, waiting, the air crackling between us. My hand is still buried in her hair; her hands are by her sides.

Her words run hot over my lips. "We're using each other, Lucas."

I shift the tiniest amount, grazing a kiss over her lower lip. She follows, seeking more, but I pull back. "Okay, then let's use each other."

Her hand comes up, gently stroking my beard. I close my eyes, her soft touch soothing me like nothing else. Thank God she's touching me.

"I think this is a very bad idea," she whispers right before she kisses me. And she's not gentle, kissing roughly, her hands tugging my hair, nipping my lower lip. Is this angry sex with Alice? Sign me up.

She grabs my shirt and attempts to rip it open. She pulls

back and stares at it. "Your buttons were supposed to go flying."

"It's too well made for that." Though the truth is she's probably not strong enough to make it happen. "Anyway, we don't need to worry about my shirt," I say, shoving my hand up her dress and between her legs. A bold demand. I've been careful with her until now.

She gasps, her eyes wide, and then she grabs my head, kissing me passionately. *Yesss.* It's a wild kiss, all lips and tongue and teeth, her hands all over me. She's ready for more. I shove her damp panties to the side, sliding my fingers inside her, thrusting as I use my thumb to tease her, flicking back and forth. She moans in the back of her throat, every soft sound driving me on. Within minutes, she's riding my hand, her nails digging into my back.

She tears her mouth away. "Now! I need you inside me."

I don't hesitate, ripping her panties off with one sharp tug, and pulling her up off the sofa. I guide her to the side, bend her over the top, yank her dress up and bunch it at her lower back. My cock surges thick and hard against my trousers.

"Ohhh!" she exclaims as I'm freeing myself, in too much of a hurry to completely undress. "This is just like—ah!"

I couldn't take it slow. I'm in deep, and I need this. I pound into her, my eyes closing over the intense sensation. Jesus. I have to slow down. This is Alice. Sweet, gentle Alice.

She arches her hips back into me. "More," she demands.

And I give it to her. I can't help myself. Can't stop. It's wild and animal and sweaty. I'm panting, trying to hang on. *Not yet, not yet.* Fuck. I reach around and stroke her firmly. She cries out and then she tightens around me, pushing me closer to the edge. I still, deep inside her, and focus on her release, gentling my touch, teasing her until she's begging in a litany of desperate needy pleas. "Lucas, I need, I need. Give. Me."

I clamp my teeth on the side of her neck as I cover her, thrusting deep, my fingers stroking exactly the way I know sets her off. She stiffens, clamping down around me, and I nearly roar with triumph. She comes violently, rocking under me, her body squeezing me rhythmically. Fu-u-uck. I grab her tight and pump deep over and over, my own harsh breath mingling with her soft cries. And then I explode in a rush of pleasure, light flashing behind my closed eyelids.

I open my eyes slowly and straighten, running my hand up her spine to the nape of her neck and giving her a squeeze. She's limp and languid. I've never let go like that with her. I've focused on her pleasure, on treating her better than her past lovers. I didn't want to be an animal pounding away mindlessly.

I withdraw and look at her still bent over the back of the sofa, eerily quiet. Fuck. Was I too rough?

I shift to get a better look at her. Her head is turned away. "Alice?"

She turns toward me, her cheeks flushed pink, eyes bright, and she smiles. Pure euphoria surges through me at that sweet smile. I do love her. It must be real if her smile can do this to me. She straightens, turns to me, and wobbles a bit. I reach out to steady her, and she wraps her arms around my neck.

She kisses me. "That was just like *The Duke's Dare* when he took her over the back of the settee."

I'm thrown for a moment. She's right, but that's not why I did it. I just needed her badly. "Did I…was I too rough?"

She shakes her head with a smile. "No. Was it better for you that way?"

"I like it all ways with you."

She strokes my beard. "I think you should let go as much as you want. I'm not fragile."

"I didn't want to be like your disappointing hookups. I imagine they took what they wanted and left."

"Yes, but you give." She pats my cheek. "Besides, they just wanted the regular position."

I smile. "It's called missionary."

She looks to the ceiling, her lips pursed. "That must have

an interesting history. Missionary. I should look into that." She meets my eyes. "Do you mind if I go back to my story?"

I push down the hurt that she wants her laptop more than me. If that's the case, then I need to work harder to increase my appeal. "Actually, I do. I have plans for you." Then I scoop her up, cradled in my arms, and carry her to the bedroom.

She sighs, pressing her cheek against my chest. *This. This is all I need.* Well, maybe just one more thing. "Will you go to the site visit with me? It would help so much."

Her fingers trace my bicep. "Okay, one more time as your fiancée and that's it."

An alarm rings in the dim recesses of my mind. What happens after the game is over? Could we have a future? Or will she move on to the next lover, her next inspiration? The irony is not lost on me. I'm the man who's always moving on to the next woman.

I don't know how I got in so deep so fast. It's been a little over a week. Maybe it was her vulnerability that drew me in, the way she leaned on me. I'm so rarely the one people lean on. I've cultivated my partying rep for so long that people don't see a man of substance behind it. Alice did. And she supported me too in my business venture. Her confidence in me has been a huge boon.

I set her down on the bed, and she opens her arms to me with a sweet, gentle smile that wraps around my heart. All this time I chose hard jaded women, the kind who were more like me, when it was the opposite I needed.

I cover her, nuzzling into her neck, breathing in her sweet flowery scent as her arms close around me. She's mine. The woman meant for me. I have never been so certain of anything in my life.

I just need to make her believe it.

~

Alice

I'm in a Mercedes with Lucas, driving down the long palace road to meet Jules and his colleague David at the dock, where they're due to arrive shortly by ferry. A guard, Michael —though I prefer to think of him as Thor—is in the front passenger seat, along with a driver. There's another Mercedes behind us for our visitors. We'll be meeting Anna and Gabriel over at the day spa for the tour. Lucas wants to show the bankers the setup by the dock in an old warehouse, where they've been developing the cosmetics line. He hopes to convert more of the buildings there to manufacturing, along with building something new. Many of the buildings formerly used by the fishermen are empty due to declining fish populations.

I'm nervous, ridiculously so. I'd like to think it's because I haven't seen Gabriel since the family dinner, where he made it clear Lucas would lose his place in the business if our fake engagement is found out. But the truth is, deep down, I'm just plain scared. Lucas has been…a dream. Ever since our fight two days ago, he's been all over me, and I don't mean that just in the sexual way, though he has been that. Decadently so. But he's also been extremely affectionate and piling on the princely manners that I've always dreamed of. I've forgiven him his deception because he truly spoke from the heart, all with good intentions toward me. And my blackened heart is beating anew with every look from him, every touch, every crooked sexy smile.

I'm falling for him.

My stupid romantic heart overrides every ounce of sense I possess. I want to be hard and practical. Realistically, I know I'm not ready for love again so soon. And I don't know if he has those kinds of deep feelings for me. Maybe he's like this with every woman and that's why he's known for his charm. I only have to Google his name to see all the women who love him—the women he's been with and the women who dream of being with him, stalking him online.

I stare at the cute white cottages we pass, trying to make sense of my time with Lucas. I got what I wanted, a story and, at long last, my writing mojo. I'm going to have the first draft done by the end of the week just in time to email it to my editor before leaving for my London book signing. From London, I could go back home, finish up revisions, and send the final draft to my editor. Or I could stay in my palace suite for the additional four weeks Anna granted me free of charge. There is something to be said for palace life. My every need is attended to, freeing up all my energy and time for writing. But that means more time with Lucas, and I don't know if it's smart to let myself get further entangled with the world's most eligible royal bachelor. I need to be smarter about relationships—ease into things, protect my heart, and have an escape plan.

Escape plan? How unromantic. Obviously, my heart still has scars.

Lucas takes my hand, entwining our fingers. "You're awfully quiet."

"I'm nervous about how this is going to go today," I say, giving him part of the truth. "I don't want to further aggravate King Gabriel."

"Just follow Prince Lucas's lead," he says, giving me his crooked smile, his aquamarine eyes sparkling with amusement. My heart thumps harder, my stomach doing a topsy-turvy dance, every nerve ending alert and aware. How does that smile provoke a stronger reaction every time? It's not like I haven't seen it before.

I focus on his eyes, his stunning aquamarine eyes. "After this meeting, I need to go into my writing cave to finish my draft. I only have three days before I leave for London, and I need to turn it in before I leave. It's a hard deadline from my publisher."

He lifts our joined hands and brushes a kiss over my knuckles, his eyes intent on mine. "Is this your polite way of asking me to give you some space?"

I flush guiltily. I guess it was, in part, because I'm scared and I'm falling for him and I don't know what to do about it.

"I'll text you at the end of each day once my brain is completely fried and out of words, if you want to visit me."

His big hand cups the back of my neck, drawing me close, his words running hot over my lips. "I'll do more than visit you, sweet Alice. I will ravish you."

My breath shudders out, my pulse thrumming through my veins. He hits every button of mine—romantic terms of endearment, Regency speak, princely manners that I've *never* experienced outside of a book, and a sexual prowess that makes me a greedy multi-orgasmic fiend for more.

He gives me a swift hard kiss before shifting to my ear, his voice a husky rumble, "And by ravish I mean fuck you senseless and then make you *beg* for more." I shiver at his words, and then he gets more explicit, the words feeding my overactive imagination until I picture it so vividly I'm throbbing with need, my breath quickening, hot all over. And he hasn't even touched me.

And then he does, his hand sliding between my legs under the cover of my dress. I jolt and shove his hand away. "Lucas!" I hiss. We're not in a limo with a closed divider. It's a car, and the driver and guard are *right there* in the front seat.

He grins. "What?" Then he whispers, "It'll relax you."

The car stops moving, and the driver says without turning around, "We're here, Your Highness, ma'am."

Lucas holds my jaw and kisses me. "Another time." He peers out the window. "The ferry isn't here yet. We'll take a short walk near the dock."

He helps me out of the car, takes my hand, and guides me to a footpath just before the dock. Thor follows behind us, the driver returning to the car.

"Alice, relax," Lucas says, giving my hand a squeeze. "It's going to go smooth as silk today."

"I am relaxed," I say tightly.

"Maybe we should head back to the privacy of the car," he says with a leer. "I'll ask the driver to take a walk."

I shake my head, my pulse skyrocketing at his way of relaxing me. "Consider me taken care of in that department."

We've been plenty busy in the bedroom, and I draw the line at fucking in the backseat of a car in broad daylight. At least I have a line.

He smirks and then he guides me down a path to the beach, drawing me closer to the hypnotic waves. A cool breeze washes over me, bringing the salty tang of sea air. Something in me relaxes.

He stops, wraps his arms around my waist from behind me, and I melt into his warm embrace. "It's fortunate the sea soothes you since we're on an island."

"I've always wanted to live near the water," I confess.

"Then you should."

"If wishes were millions of dollars…"

"Stay with me."

"What?"

He turns me toward him. "Stay with me here on Villroy."

"What are you saying?" I back up a step, my stomach dropping. "What are you saying?" My voice is high and reedy because some part of me knows, and I can't go there. I take another step back, my pumps shifting in the sand, making me stumble.

He grabs me by the upper arms and guides me back to him. "Okay, calm down. You look like you're in a horror movie. It is not that bad."

"I'm not ready," I manage over the lump in my throat.

He turns me back to the sea, his hands on my shoulders. "Breathe. Look at the sea and breathe. Forget I said that. You are my fake fiancée and, after this, you're going back to your suite to finish your story."

I slowly relax again. Somehow he knows just what I need to hear, even when he's the one who caused my distress.

He kisses the side of my neck before speaking low in my ear, "But I think you know you're mine now. I'll give you some time to get used to it."

Arrogant domineering man. I turn, glaring at him. His crooked smile appears right on cue, his blue-green eyes soft. "I'll wait, Alice."

My knees go weak. I open my mouth and shut it again, unsure if I want to blast him for his arrogance or admit I'm in deep and I'm terrified. Maybe he knows I'm in deep. Or maybe he just assumes that I will fall in line with his plan to keep me. Does he love me?

A horn bellows and we both look over at the approaching ferry. "Showtime," he says, grabbing my hand and tucking it in the crook of his elbow, guiding me off the beach.

My nerves are shot. From worry over the meeting today to Lucas proposing I live on Villroy, I literally cannot deal with one more thing. So I let him take the lead, following him blindly back to the waiting cars on the road next to the dock. The driver will guide our guests to the second car. *Our guests? His* guests.

"Lucas, when you say that I'm yours, is that your arrogant domineering way of saying you l-like me a lot, or maybe feel like…"

He stops and frames my face with his hands. "I love you."

"Oh!" My eyes water, my chin wobbling. "Oh." He's shocked the words right out of me. Somehow I hadn't expected an open admission of deep feelings, the kind I've been drowning in for the past few days.

He kisses me tenderly. "I'll wait for you to catch up."

I stare at his chest. "I'm already there, and it terrifies me." My voice cracks, and I feel so out of sorts I can't move. Maybe I don't want to move.

His hands slide down my shoulders to my elbows and then wrap around me, his mouth covering mine in a passionate kiss. I wrap my arms around his neck, losing myself in the kiss and everything he makes me feel. It is the kiss that tops all other kisses, and I never want it to end.

Even when people start cheering and whistling.

Even when Lucas's hands cup my ass and press me against him.

Even when I hear my name.

Wait. I know that voice. I jerk away from Lucas, turn, and face my worst nightmare—Mason.

And Riley.

Here on Villroy.

My hand flies to my chest, my heart racing. I break out into a cold sweat, and my world does a horrific spin, making me sway on my feet. Lucas's hand closes over my upper arm, keeping me steady. He's talking to me, but I can't make sense of the words.

I blink a few times, hardly believing my eyes. Mason and Riley are *here* on Villroy. What are they doing here?

I look away, trying to think. They're not supposed to be here. They're intruding on my solo honeymoon that I paid for with my own hard-earned cash. And they're interrupting the most romantic moment of my life!

A red haze fills my vision, and when I finally speak, there's so much venom in my voice I barely recognize myself. "I will *kill* him. Mason is here, and he brought Riley."

"Hell," Lucas says. "I'll help you kill him, but this is not the time. Come on. Let's get to the cars. Jules and David are already there."

He practically drags me away, his arm around my shoulders.

Footsteps pound behind us. "Wait!" Mason yells. "Alice, Riley needs to talk to you."

"Go away!" I shout over my shoulder.

Lucas drops his hold on me, turns, and stalks toward Mason. Riley remains standing a short distance away. She looks disgustingly cute with her long black hair up in a high ponytail, wearing a white tank top with dark orange capris and high-heeled sandals. I bet she paid for the expensive plane tickets. Her family is loaded.

I catch up to Lucas just in time to hear him say in a commanding voice of authority, "You two wait here. A car will drive you to the palace, where you will then wait in the entrance hall until Alice and I have time for you." He turns to Thor. "Call ahead and have two guards on them at all times."

"Who are you?" Mason asks Lucas, his brows drawn together.

"Do as you're told," Lucas snaps, "or you will be escorted right back to the ferry and off this island forever."

Mason turns to me. "Alice, what's going on? Did you bring another man on our honeymoon?"

I gasp. The nerve! After what he did?

Lucas grabs Mason by the shirt and hauls him up close. "Not another word." He throws Mason back from him, and Mason stumbles. "And I'm the fucking prince of Villroy and Alice's fiancé."

"Alice?" Mason asks like he's totally lost.

Lucas wraps his arm around my shoulders and guides me to the car. I'm shaking with fury, my mind racing at everything I want to spew at Mason and Riley for daring to show up here at the place that was supposed to be my retreat away from all the hurt they put me through.

But there's no time for spewing the venom building inside me because there's Jules and David.

Lucas smiles and calls, "*Bonjour!*" along with more warm and cheerful French. I paste on a smile, not even blinking when Lucas introduces me as his fiancée.

My worlds are colliding, and there's too many fiancés, real and fake, for my tender heart to take.

16

———

Lucas

I will kill him. I swear to God. Just when I finally connect with Alice—she loves me, by some miracle she loves me, even after a devastating breakup that would've closed most people's hearts for a good long time—*he* shows up, reminding her of all the hurt that giving your heart to someone can bring. Talk about one step forward, one giant leap back. She's nearly catatonic by my side at the day spa. On the ride over, I urged her to go back to her room to give her a break from the pressure of the business meeting. I'd just tell everyone she's not feeling well. She refused, saying flatly, "Nope. I'm a badass." As if that moniker will protect her. I know her. She's a sweet, tender soul. And even a badass needs a safe space to retreat before all hell breaks loose.

What the fuck is he doing here? And why, of all that is holy, did he bring Riley, the supposed best friend who stabbed Alice in the back?

I blow out a breath. Anna is giving the bankers the tour, the rest of us following behind. It seems to be going well. Both Jules and David are impressed with what we've done here, and Anna's natural enthusiasm really sells it.

"You mentioned a possible restaurant in addition to the

spa's café?" David asks once we've circled back to the lobby. The conversation has remained in English after Anna's initial *"Bonjour, Monsieurs!"* made them wince. Her pronunciation is atrocious. Though, in her defense, she's had little time with her French tutor, and Gabriel only teaches her dirty words. Something she shared with me when I first asked after her lessons a couple of months ago.

"Yes," Anna says. "The restaurant menu would feature seafood fresh caught by our fishermen. Maybe we'll get a French chef. They're the best."

"We do like our food," Jules says amiably.

"Let me show you where the restaurant would go," she says, pointing toward the side exit.

We all file out, looking at the flat land overlooking the sea. Gabriel takes over, catching them up with what we've put into the project so far financially and what we project to bring in, even without the restaurant.

"Yes," David murmurs, glancing at me. "Your CFO has already filled us in on the numbers."

Gabriel's gaze lands on me with a brief nod of acknowledgment before shifting to Alice at my side and looking away. He doesn't understand about Alice. The engagement is fake, but the love is real. And when Alice is ready, whenever that is, we'll take that next step to the real thing. I never thought I'd be excited about the possibility of an engagement. I used to find the mere idea of marriage repulsive. That was before sweet Alice. I take her hand, and it's ice cold despite the warm June day. She's staring at the sea, completely closed in on herself. Probably deep in the refuge of her imagination.

I will deal with her ex, and then I'll help her through this. She shouldn't have to go through the hell of dealing with the double betrayal all over again. I play out various scenarios in my mind for how best to deal with him, but I can't find one that doesn't end in violence. I want to punch him so bad I can taste it. I know Alice wouldn't want that. She's a nonviolent soul. Even when she was freshly reeling from his betrayal, she still had a kind word to say about him. She never even blocked him from her phone, much to my aggravation. I have to keep a clear head for her sake.

I tune back in to the conversation just as Gabriel says, "Please join us at the palace for luncheon."

"Of course," Jules says with a wide smile. "I've never seen your ancestral home."

David actually cracks a smile. "We would be delighted."

Alice grips my arm tightly, her alarmed gaze alerting me to the problem. Mason and Riley are waiting in the entrance hall. All of our guests pass through that way. "I'll call ahead and have our uninvited guests moved," I whisper in her ear.

She nods in a jerky motion, her expression pale and strained. "To the dungeon," she whispers.

She doesn't smile at her joke like she normally does, but it makes me feel better that she's sounding more like herself. I kiss her cheek. Still no smile, but she shoots me a tender look.

As soon as I'm in the privacy of our car, I arrange for the guards to move Mason and Riley to the private salon immediately. I want them there because it's a good distance past the dining room, so there's no chance of them popping out of the room and spotting us. I don't care how long they wait.

When we arrive at the palace courtyard, Alice and I wait a few moments in the car for confirmation that Mason and Riley are in the salon. Once we get it, I help her out of the car and tuck her hand in my elbow, guiding her through the courtyard.

A servant opens the door for us, and we step inside to find the rest of our group chatting cheerfully.

"We're heading to the private salon for a celebratory drink," Gabriel says to me. "Luncheon won't be ready for another hour."

No! "Let's go to the rooftop garden instead," I say smoothly. "It's a beautiful day, and I'm sure Jules and David would enjoy the view." I turn to Jules and David. "You can see the whole island from up there."

"Perhaps after luncheon," Gabriel replies. "I offered our guests my finest scotch, which is in the salon."

I work hard to keep the panic from my voice because I know that with Mason in the picture, this fake engagement will absolutely blow up in my face, and then I'll be out of the business for good. Not to mention the effect all this will have on Alice. "We'll bring the scotch to the roof."

Gabriel's eyes narrow, his jaw tight. "And we'll also be signing the paperwork. I don't want papers flying in the breeze up on the rooftop. What is wrong with the salon?"

"Nothing." I smile. "Sounds fantastic."

As soon as we move for drinks, I stride ahead, hoping to find a servant along the way who can move Mason and Riley ahead of our arrival. Alice grabs my hand in a death grip, which slows me down, and then before I can tell her my plan to flag down a servant, Jules is at her side.

"Alice," he says, "my wife and her friends were thrilled with their signed books. Celeste would love to see you again, and more of her friends are asking after you. Do you ever come to Paris for a book signing?"

Alice smiles and replies with real warmth in her voice, which would be a relief if I wasn't dying to intercept the waiting catastrophe. "I would love that, but I don't have any Paris signings planned in the immediate future."

I don't wait around for Jules's response, instead loosening my hand from Alice's grip and striding ahead of the group to find a servant. Suddenly Anna is at my side, her arm linking with mine. She moves fast, her long legs easily matching my stride. I can't bring myself to wrench away from my heavily pregnant sister-in-law.

"Somebody is in love," she teases in a soft voice.

"I am," I say, unable to help my smile. "And she is too."

"Oh, Lucas! I'm so happy for you both." She lowers her voice. "You can say it, this was all my doing."

"It was mostly my devastating charm."

She laughs. "I like her. I really do. Will she be staying here on Villroy?"

"I don't know. She's still skittish and her ex just showed up. He's in the damn salon. I've been trying to direct Gabriel away from it, but he's impossible."

She halts in her tracks. "Gabriel?" she calls. "I'm feeling a little light-headed. I think I'm going to lie down."

Gabriel nearly knocks me down in his rush to get to her side. "What is it? Is it the baby? Are you in labor?"

"No, it's not that," she says quickly. "I just need to rest. Would you mind walking me back to our suite? Lucas can entertain our guests until you return." She sends me a pointed look. She is good.

"Of course," Gabriel says, wrapping an arm around her. "And I'll call for the doctor just to check in."

"No doctor," Anna says firmly.

Gabriel quietly takes his leave of Jules and David, promising to return once Anna is settled. He insists his guard accompany them and remain posted outside her door. He loves her with a fierce devotion that I'm only beginning to understand. I watch for a moment as he guides Anna ahead of us, turning toward the stairs that lead to their suite. They have a low intense conversation as they walk. Gabriel is probably adamant on the need for a doctor, and Anna is just as adamant that it's not necessary. She took the heat for me. I owe her for that and more.

I join Jules, David, and Alice again. "Would you like to see the gardens? It's just through here in the courtyard."

"Actually, I was really looking forward to that scotch," Jules says.

"Of course," I murmur. Now that Gabriel and Anna have left, I have no way of dashing off to find a servant without being obvious.

Jules is warm and cordial, chatting away in French to me, David chiming in, Alice utterly silent. I would insist on switching back to English for Alice's sake, but I don't think she's up to conversation right now. Disaster is waiting for us in the salon—we both know it—and she looks like she wants to bolt.

"Alice," I say during a brief pause in the conversation, "would you like to meet up with us for luncheon in a bit? I know you're on a very tight book deadline."

Her head snaps up. "Yes. My brain has really been cranking, and I'm dying to write it all down."

"The *auteur*!" Jules exclaims. "Of course you must express your art. Us men will drink our scotch while you work your magic."

"Thank you!" She hurries off, and I nearly sag with relief.

Now I don't have to worry about a big scene with Mason and Riley upsetting Alice. I'll just ask the guards posted outside the salon to escort them back to the entrance hall and all will be well.

By the time we reach the salon, I'm in much better spirits. After all, we're about to sign the loan that I helped bring about, and everything is going according to plan. Even better, I found the love of my life.

I stop in front of the guards, Louis and Claude, posted outside the door. "Please escort them back to the entrance hall to wait for me there." I wait while they go in to retrieve Mason and Riley.

"Just a moment," I tell Jules and David. "I've had a couple of unexpected visitors and, unfortunately, it's not looking to be a pleasant visit. Nothing serious. Just a misunderstanding I need to deal with after our business is concluded."

David's brows shoot up. Jules looks concerned, but quickly says, "Of course."

The salon door opens, Claude stepping outside with us, Louis trailing behind Mason and Riley. The moment Mason spots me, he says, "Hey! We've waited long enough! I didn't travel all this way just to be given the runaround! I want to see Alice. Where is she?"

He stops in front of me, glowering in an attempt to look threatening, but I know what kind of man he is. He cheats and lies. He's a coward. "What have you done with her?"

I hold the guards off because I need him to understand something. "She's mine."

He becomes even more agitated. Maybe I'll get to punch him after all. "Where's Alice?" he barks. "I have a right to see my fiancée!"

Riley pipes up, appearing at his side. "She's not your fiancée anymore! I am!"

"She's *my* fiancée," I say through clenched teeth. "And you need to wait in the entrance hall."

"Lucas, what is going on here?" Jules asks.

I close my eyes. In my aggravation, I nearly forgot Jules and David were here.

"Ha!" Mason barks. "There is no way Alice would get engaged again that quickly. We just ended our engagement a few weeks ago. She doesn't rush anything; slow and careful, that's Alice."

I'm about to defend our rush engagement by saying it was love at first sight, which is only a slight stretch of the truth, when I hear Alice's voice behind me, slightly out of breath.

"I got lost."

I turn, wondering how much she heard.

Jules and David step back, allowing Alice to step forward.

She gazes into my eyes, her voice steadier. "The palace is so big I got lost." She looks over my shoulder. "I heard your voice, Mason, and I followed it back here to tell you this—I don't know why you're here and I don't care. I gave you my heart, and you weren't careful with it. You stabbed me in the back, straight through my heart, and then you *twisted the knife*—" she bares her teeth and twists an imaginary knife "—by being with my best friend. In one bloody, devastating swoop you took everything that meant some-thing to me! You, Riley, my ability to write my favorite uplifting stories in the world—all gone!" She looks to the ceiling, blinking rapidly, and my own eyes sting in empathy.

She stares at him, and I stare at her, watching carefully in case she needs me. "I thought I might die," she says quietly. "But I didn't. I cried, I railed against the unfairness of it all, and then I got myself here for a much-needed refuge from all reminders of you and Riley."

She meets my eyes. "I met Lucas." She smiles, her sweet gentle smile, and my chest constricts, my throat tight with emotion. "I found my inspiration." She turns to Mason, lifting her chin. "I'm writing again. And I've found love with a man who treats me the way I deserve. So-o-o, that's it." She nods once, brightening. "You and Riley need to leave. There's nothing more I have to say to either of you, nothing more I would ever give, so goodbye."

My lips curve in a small smile. I'm so damn proud of her. "That was badass." She told me she was a badass the first time we met. Back then she was barely holding it together, trying to be a badass. Now she really is.

She beams. "Thank you."

"Riley needs to talk to you," Mason blurts.

I turn to glare at Mason. Does the man have a death wish?

Riley rushes forward. "Alice, I feel so awful about the way things went down. I didn't mean to fall in love with him. It just happened, and I'm so, so sorry. I hope one day you'll forgive me. I miss you so much. You're the family I chose, and I can't bear to know you'll never be in my life again."

Alice's lips form a flat line.

Mason cuts in. "Alice, she loves you. She can't sleep at night. She's wrecked over it. That's why I keep calling and texting you. She said you wouldn't talk to her, but I thought if I could just explain how terrible she feels, you'd consider it. I know how close you two are."

"How close we *were*," Alice says.

"I really am sorry," Riley says in a small voice, her eyes welling.

We all look to Alice for her reaction.

She sighs. "You know what I wish?"

"What?" Riley asks, sounding hopeful.

Alice replies in a clear strong voice. "I wish for you and Mason to discover what cheating liars you both are. Riley, Mason will cheat and lie again. And, Mason, I fully expect

Riley to do the same. Cheating liars are never satisfied. They're always looking for the next, better thing, trying to fill that hole within themselves, but guess what? That hole will never be filled because it's an ugly festering wound made of your own insecurities and deeply flawed character. I hope you hurt each other as much as you hurt me. That's my wish." She turns to Louis waiting patiently behind Riley. "Hercules, take them away!"

"Ma'am, my name is Louis. And I would be happy to." He inclines his head for Riley to exit the room, and she does, her head hanging low, shoulders drooped in defeat. Mason has to be encouraged to go with a firm hold on his arm by the other guard.

I pull Alice into my arms and kiss the top of her head. "Well done, my darling badass."

She looks up at me, giving me her sweet smile. "I can't believe I finally got to say all that. I was in such shock before I couldn't."

Jules clears his throat.

"Oh, I am so sorry, Jules," I say. "You too, David, that you had to witness our personal issues. Please, let's have that drink now."

"On the contrary," David says. "I found it fascinating."

Jules nods. "Did you and Alice really get engaged after only knowing each other a few weeks?"

I turn to Alice, a question in my eyes. After all the emotional upheaval of confronting Mason and Riley, does she still want to be my fiancée? I want that for real this time.

She lifts her ruby ring. "We did."

Her voice is measured, not precisely down, but I know her, and she's not truly happy at the prospect. She's smoothing the way for me in my business transaction. She's not ready for an engagement. I need to be patient.

"How wonderful," Jules says. "A romantic thing for a romance writer to do."

She stares at her ring. "Yes, it is."

"Let's get those drinks," I say brightly and lead the way,

heading to the wet bar to pour. Alice walks by my side while Jules and David take a seat on the burgundy leather sofa.

I pour the first tumbler, and Alice grabs it, tossing it back. "You okay?" I ask.

"I need to get back to work," she says grimly. "I'm not losing my job over those two. I need to finish the draft."

"Wait." I pull her close, sliding my arm around her waist, and dip my head near her ear. "I'll join you in a bit. Give yourself a little time. That was an ordeal."

She goes up on tiptoe to whisper, "No. The Ordeal is behind me, and now I'm moving forward."

I have to admire her fortitude. "Okay. I'll call for Christina to escort you to your suite." I kiss her cheek and add in a low voice, "Thank you for all you've done."

Gabriel returns just then and joins Jules and David. I go through the motions, pouring drinks, and joining in on the toast, but my heart isn't in it.

It's with Alice as she stands by my side, feeling thousands of miles away.

She's got my heart, and I can only hope she'll stay with me. My gut churns. Somehow it feels less like a sure thing than it did before Mason and Riley's arrival.

17

―――――――――

Alice

I spent the last three days in a marathon writing session, and I'm thrilled to have my story in a good place. First draft done! I can breathe now. Yay me! I did it! I met my deadline. I smile to myself, click save once more for good luck, and close out of the document. Then I click on my email and send it off to my editor and cc her boss. Of course, that's not the final version, but the shape of it is there. Author job secured. Well, it will be once I turn in the final draft in four weeks.

I stand and stretch; then I walk over to the bed, spread my arms wide, and fall back on it. Ahh. It's Saturday night. I should pack for my London book signing tomorrow, but I'm just going to enjoy my moment. Nothing beats finishing a first draft. Other than typing *The End*, that is. I save that for the final version.

Oh, I should text Quinn the good news! I scoot up toward the nightstand, grab my phone and text her. *First draft is done! Just emailed it to you.*

Quinn replies a moment later. It's still early in New York. *Got it! I'll read it this weekend.*

Be gentle, okay? It's not pretty. Normally, she only sees the final version, but my extremely late deadline made the publisher nervous. I have to send the first draft and the final draft to keep my contract. Right now, my story is an ill-behaved ugly thing, but it's *my* ill-behaved ugly thing. Only I can truly love it.

Quinn: *I won't even comment. I'll just read.*

I smile and text back a quick "thanks" with a cute emoji of a smiley face with black glasses like me.

She responds with multiple book emojis in a row, which is the only emoji she ever uses. Quinn is a very dignified, sophisticated fifty-something New Yorker, after all. Ha-ha. I had to show her the book emoji, but she really took to it.

I let out a happy sigh. Then I text Lucas. *I finished my draft! Could you play with my hair and call me darling?*

Be right there.

I smile. He doesn't even bat an eye at my request. I asked him to play with my hair a few nights ago when I was still fresh from the Mason-Riley confrontation or, as I'm now calling it, The Badass Show. Even a badass enjoys the soothing pleasure of having her hair played with. Lucas was new to the concept but took to it beautifully. And now that we're done playing the fake fiancée game, I asked him to put my ruby ring back in the vault, where it belongs. I confess it's a relief. Once real feelings got involved, the engagement part made me feel panicky. I'm just not ready. Only two weeks ago, I was supposed to be walking down the aisle with another man.

I sit up. I'm still in my pajamas—a loose sleep shirt and shorts. Maybe I should try to look presentable. Of course, the last few nights when I texted Lucas to visit, it was past midnight and I was already in bed in my pajamas, so it's not like he hasn't seen me like this. Though he stripped me out of my pajamas almost as soon as he got in bed. But tonight it's earlier, way before midnight. I head over to the closet, thinking of wearing a dress because I might actually leave my writing cave. It's Saturday and I've basically been holed up here since Wednesday.

I pick out a light blue wrap dress that brings out my eyes,

toss it on the bed, and decide I should shower as well. I already did this morning, but I was in too much of a hurry to wash my hair. I text Lucas my plans so he'll know I need some extra time. Three dots appear like he's typing, and then a moment later, I'm staring at the unexpected.

I'm the one who plays with your hair, so I should be the one who washes it.

My pulse thrums through my veins. This will be a first. Lucas has still been asleep when I've had my morning shower. When I've got a story burning through me, I get up early, my mind a cacophony of character voices needing to be part of things. I always honor that gift by typing out what I hear immediately, but then it doesn't always fall in place in the story right away, so I shower, caffeinate, and return to them. All that to say, shower sex is new to me with Lucas, with anyone. Not that I haven't imagined it. My ex wouldn't even try because he thought he might get chilly if I took up all the space under the showerhead. *He's all yours, Riley!*

I try to come up with something suitably sexy to text back in response, but I'm so busy picturing exactly how this is going to work that I don't quite get to it. The thing is, it's a one-person shower, though there is a bench and a handheld sprayer thingy, so I could straddle him on the bench or maybe I could stand with him behind me or, knowing Lucas, he'll want to show off his strength and lift me for standing sex, but I'll worry about his back that way. As strong as he is, I'm not that light. Hmmm, I need a visual.

I set my phone back on the nightstand, march into the bathroom, and eye the shower. Maybe I should get it started so it's nice and steamy in there. The last thing I want is to hear Lucas complain about getting chilly, like some wimps I know. I turn on the water and resume my shower sexual-positioning scenarios. That handheld shower thingy has real possibilities. What if—

"Darling."

I jump and whirl to face him, my hand at my throat. "Lucas! You scared me! Don't sneak up on me like that!"

He laughs. "I didn't sneak. I knocked on the bedroom door, you didn't hear me, then I called your name on my way in here." His lips curve into a knowing smirk. "What were you imagining in that dirty mind of yours?"

I smooth my hair, feigning innocence. "Who said I was imagining dirty things?"

He pulls me into his arms, his hand sliding under my hair to cup the back of my neck. His words run hot over my lips. "When are you not imagining dirty things?"

I don't answer because I want his kiss more than I want to pretend I was innocently preparing a shower. Instead I wrap my arms around his waist and tip my face up to his.

He smiles against my lips and then he kisses me, gently at first, a soft brush back and forth, a teasing invitation. I open for him on a sigh, and he deepens the kiss, his large hand splayed on the small of my back, his fingers heating my skin through the thin fabric of my sleep shirt. My knees go weak, and I wrap my arms around his neck, melting against him, lost in the haze of a drugging passionate kiss.

He becomes more aggressive, wrapping my hair around his fist, his mouth hungry, his hand sliding to my ass, pressing me firmly against him in a hold that says *you're mine*. He wants to possess me, keep me, make me his forever. I see it in his smoldering eyes, feel it in his heated touch, hear it in his gravelly voice. And I give him as much as I can. I hold back nothing, but I don't promise forever. And he doesn't ask.

He breaks the kiss, his eyes dark with desire. "Take off your clothes." His voice holds the soft edge of authority.

I hand him my glasses, strip off my sleep shirt, and take my glasses back, holding both shirt and glasses. "You're my first shower sex."

His smile lights up his face. "Is that so?"

"Yes." I set my stuff on the long bathroom counter and turn. Luckily, he's moved right behind me, so I'm not trying to find him through a blur. He takes my hand and guides me back, closer to the shower. "So I was trying to imagine what position…" I trail off as my sleep shorts are suddenly around my ankles.

Lucas is on his knees in front of me and helps me step out of them. "I knew you were imagining dirty things. I love that about you." He leans forward and kisses me through my panties. I'm instantly wet. "Sweet Alice," he murmurs in approval, pressing another hot kiss against me before hooking his fingers in the sides of the silky fabric and sliding them off.

My breath hitches as his hand slowly slides up my inner thigh, his lips following in a tingling path. His fingers part me, and then his tongue drags across me. "Lucas," I moan, my hips arching, my fingers tangling in his hair. Nothing is better than Lucas's mouth on me.

His powerful hands clamp on my hips, holding me in place and supporting my weak knees at the same time as he claims me with his hungry mouth. I surrender to the fiery pleasure, my head dropping back, my eyes closing. It's exquisite sensual torture, locked in his hold, the fire of Lucas consuming me, pushing me closer and closer to the brink. My breath comes in short pants, my insides coiling tight and hot.

A harsh cry rips from my throat as an explosion of plea-sure rocks through my core, sending shockwaves of sensation through my entire body. He stays with me, drawing it out until I go limp.

He rises to his feet and kisses me tenderly. His voice is rough as his hands cup my breasts, caressing them. "You're so beautiful, so sexy."

I smile, stroking his soft beard. "You are a wonderful man." I'm dopey with endorphins, loose and languid.

He grabs my hand and kisses my knuckles, his eyes intent on mine. "Shower time," he says hoarsely, pulling me into the shower stall and shutting the glass door behind us.

"So how's this going to work?" I ask.

"Very well," he says with a devilish smile before pinning me against the wall and kissing me breathless. I slide my hands over his slick skin as the water runs over him, loving the play of muscle in his back. He shifts, kissing along the line of my jaw, then over to my neck, all while his hands roam from my breasts straight down to pleasure central. I gasp as his fingers thrust inside me. His mouth covers mine in a demanding kiss. I clutch his shoulders, weak and drugged by desire. And then his fingers shift to exactly where I need him, moving in slow, lazy circles. I arch into his hand, my soft cries swallowed by his mouth as the pressure builds inside me.

I tremble, I ache, I need.

And then I'm right there, teetering on the edge. "Lucas," I gasp.

His voice is gruff in my ear. "Not yet."

He lifts me before I have my wits about me, his tongue thrusting in my mouth as he thrusts deep inside me, taking me to the hilt, the ache suddenly filled. I scramble to wrap my arms and legs around him as he drives into me fiercely, claiming me, possessing me. I kiss him back passionately. He is mine. In this moment, he is mine. Suddenly I'm there on the edge of release, my body tightening around him.

He lifts his head, holding my jaw, his blue-green eyes burning into mine, the intensity ratcheting up.

My breath comes in short gasps. "Lucas," I beg.

He holds my jaw, keeping my gaze locked on his as he pumps hard and deep. My release slams into me, my hips bucking wildly, and then he's right there with me. His groan is low and guttural, his grip on my hips tight as he lets go, sagging against me.

His forehead touches mine, his hand holding my face, his voice gravelly. "Say you're mine, Alice."

I close my eyes. "Lucas." He hasn't said he loves me since that one time. He doesn't have to. I feel it; he feels it back. It's just that he wants more than that. He wants forever. It's still too soon for me. I open my eyes. "I'm not ready."

His jaw tightens, and he lifts me off him, shifts me under the spray, and strokes my hair back, soaking it. He takes care with me even when he's not entirely happy with me. I wish I could speed up time, fast-forward to a healed heart ready to open again fully, but it's impossible. I feel deeply. I heal slowly.

His touch is knowing, commanding even, reminding me he's claimed me. He washes my hair and then my body, turning me this way and that in the spray. His expression is serious, his eyes betraying a softness I know is hurt.

"Lucas, I'm sorry."

He kisses me and then nips my lower lip. "No. I don't want you sorry. I said I would wait for you to be ready, and I'm being impatient."

I grab the soap and wash his chest. "I'll miss you when I'm in London tomorrow."

He smiles. "You'll be back the next day. You can't take twenty-four hours without me?"

"Are you sure you can't come with me?"

"I told you I have some business to attend to."

I stick my lower lip out in a pout. "On a Sunday?"

"When you're a prince, doors open any day I say."

"I suppose that's true." And it's what gives him that edge of authority, the purview of royalty. It is hot. I wash him some more and rinse his front. He gives me his back, so I do that next. "Are you shopping?"

"No."

"What will you be doing?"

He looks over his shoulder at me. "I agreed to interview employees for the spa."

"It really is business."

"I swore to be honest with you."

My eyes sting. "Yes. I appreciate it."

He turns and wraps me in a hug. "I'll miss you too."

I press my cheek to his chest, surrounded by his strong arms, warmth, and love. Why can't this be enough?

I look up at him. "Let's just enjoy what we have now, okay? No expectations or talk of the future."

He pulls away and turns off the shower, his movements jerky as he grabs a towel and hands it to me without a word. I shiver despite the warmth of the steamy space. He's impatient and holding himself in check. It's only a matter of time before he decides to give up on me. I can feel it in my bones, yet I can't seem to get there. The scars are too fresh.

He wraps a towel around his waist and steps out of the shower, his muscles taut with tension.

"Lucas?" I whisper.

"I'm not angry," he says without turning around. "Just give me a minute." He gathers his clothes in one swoop.

"It's not you, it's me," I say urgently. I can't bear to hurt him.

He stills for a moment and then shakes his head. "Don't."

I swallow hard as he strides from the room.

Lucas

I'm wide awake at three a.m. Alice is sound asleep, curled on her side, her back cozied up against my side. I'm pushing for too much, I know, but it's impossible for me to contain myself. I've never felt so strongly about anyone before, and the uncertainty of the future is making me crazy. I need to know she's mine. I want to marry her. If I could just have *some* indication that she will ultimately commit to me, I could ease up.

My eye catches on her laptop sitting on the desk across the room. I asked her earlier if I could read her story. I was the inspiration for it, after all, along with our fake engagement. She told me she didn't want to share her first draft.

But it's about me. *I'm* the scoundrel. If I read it, I'd know how she secretly sees our future. The future she's too vulnerable to voice out loud will surely play out with her characters.

I cannot believe it's come to this. It's wrong to pry.

It's also wrong to push her too hard and scare her away.

Slowly, carefully, I slip out of bed, snag the laptop, and take it with me into the adjoining living room. It's chilly out here in just my boxer briefs. I don't want to wake her, trying to find my clothes from where I last tossed them, so I pad back into the bedroom, swipe the throw blanket off the bench at the foot of the bed, wrap it around my shoulders, and check one last time that she's asleep. She's out cold. I know she's been working around the clock to finish this draft, going to bed late, hanging with me, and then getting up early to get right to work.

Back on the sofa with the laptop, I lift the screen and tap a key. It's on, but it's password protected. I type "password" in case it's that easy. Nope. That was dumb. She loves words. She'd use a favorite word. Badass? No, that's a recent thing, I think. Regency? Nope, not that. I rub my beard, thinking hard. Something with love.

Suddenly I know. Besotted. She loves that word. She made me her besotted fiancé.

I type it in and the screen unlocks to a wallpaper image of a man in a loose flowing white shirt with tight breeches. Yes! No idea who that man is, probably a book cover model. I click over to her files, and there it is, right on top. She named it simply Scoundrel-1stdraft.

I click it open and begin to read my future.

18

Lucas

I'm still awake, fully dressed now, sitting at the desk in the bedroom next to her laptop, watching her sleep. I didn't sleep at all last night. I read through the whole story with the sick feeling of dread growing in my stomach as the scoundrel gets his comeuppance. She made me look terrible, a selfish arrogant man who seduces a vulnerable woman below his station. That is not me. I love her.

It ended horribly.

The *one* story inspired by me, starring me as the scoundrel in a fake engagement, ends with the scoundrel losing everything, including the woman he loves. She told me romance always ends with the couple together in a big happy ending. She's known for her uplifting happy stories! There was nothing happy or uplifting! A fucking tragic ending when it comes to me.

Her alarm goes off. She reaches an arm out of the covers, turns it off, and then a moment later jackknifes upright in bed, shoving her hair out of her face as she looks around. She's naked, her fantastic breasts bouncing with her movements. Even now, as gutted as I am by what she wrote, I still want her. She scrambles for her glasses on the nightstand, shoves them on, and finally her gaze lands on me.

"Today's my signing in London," she says. "You're up early."

"I never slept."

"Why?"

My jaw tightens. "I was thinking."

Her brows draw together. "Oh-kay, did you want to share what you were thinking about?"

"No." I spy her long sleep shirt on the floor, grab it, and toss it to her. "Put this on."

She does. "Thanks. Could you get some coffee and muffins up here while I shower and pack?"

"I live to serve you," I drawl, returning to my seat and resuming my staring session. Some part of me believes studying her carefully will give me a clue as to how her mysterious female mind works.

She shakes her head, muttering, "I don't know what crawled up your ass, but I'll do it myself." She calls to the servants' quarters, making her request, grabs some clothes, and dashes to the bathroom.

I wait and obsess some more over the horrible story I wish I never read. How could she write that about me after the way I treated her? I was good to her. I made more effort than I've ever made with any woman. Last night I even took her on a romantic walk on the beach and kissed her under the moonlit sky. Okay, she asked me to do those things, but I did it because I *want* to be the man of her dreams. I want to be the one she chooses forever. And it's now abundantly clear she doesn't feel the same way.

She emerges from the bathroom fully dressed a short while later, looking more awake. She crosses to me, her voice soft and uncertain. "Lucas?" She knows I'm angry, and I'm trying not to be. She can't help it if she doesn't feel the same way I do.

"I read your story."

Her eyes dart to the laptop next to me, her arms crossing

as she hugs herself. She turns back to me, brows furrowed over wide blue eyes, hurt etched in her features. "I can't believe you read my story," she whispers.

Guilt stabs at me. I hurt her. But she hurt me too. "Well, I did. And I know that the scoundrel leads her on, pretending to have real feelings for her when he never had any intention of marrying her. Now she's ruined, and no man will marry her." I can't help my accusing tone. She knows how much I want her to commit to me, yet she denies us both in real life and in her fictional world, which I know is her refuge, her joyful place. And she made me a villain.

Her jaw drops, and she shuts it with a snap. "I'm sorry, I must've missed the part where I gave you *permission* to go into my *private* files and read the story I specifically told you not to. In fact, when you asked to read it, my exact words were, 'No. I don't want to share my first draft.' Or does the word *no* not apply to princes?"

I stand, glowering down at her. "The scoundrel leaves her in the end, and then she creates a diabolical plan that leaves him in crippling debt. That's not a love story! It's a fucking tragedy."

She doesn't back away despite my harsh words. Instead, she lifts her chin. I'm both proud of her for holding her ground and completely exasperated. "Love stories can end happily or tragically."

"No. You told me you write romance, which specifically has the couple together in the end, yet you didn't write it that way this time. Why?"

Her blue eyes flash, her voice shaking with the force of her anger. "Let's talk about the real problem here. You betrayed my trust—again! First, you deliberately kept me in the dark about Gabriel being against the engagement, and I let you charm your way out of that one, but this is too far. You waited until I was asleep to invade my privacy because you knew it was wrong. Where is your honor? Where is your sense of integrity? You told me you were a man of honor, but your actions tell me I can't trust you."

"I am a man of honor!"

She scoffs. "How did you even get on my laptop? It's password protected."

My lip curls. "Besotted. Anyone who knows you could guess."

She jabs a finger in my chest. "Only you would guess because I called you that. I've never called anyone that before."

"What a compliment for me," I say in a voice dripping with sarcasm. "I get the 'besotted' when it's all a game, and now that it's real, I get nothing."

She throws her hands up. "I can't deal with you right now! I have to pack!" She yanks her suitcase out of the closet, wheels it over to the bed, and tosses it on top. Then she starts piling clothes in it. It's an overnight trip, yet she's packing everything. Is she leaving for good?

My gut churns. I'm hurt and angry and feeling a little desperate. Princes don't beg, we don't grovel, we don't chase after a woman. Why did I have to fall for the one woman who refuses to fall back?

"Go," she snaps, heading to the bathroom, probably to pack her toiletries.

I stand but I can't leave. I need answers. I need hope. I take a seat on the edge of the unmade bed, lean my elbows on my knees, and rest my head in my hands. My mind is muddled, my nerves raw, exhaustion making me even tenser.

I hear her before I see her, packing her laptop across the room, and then she's close, her flowery sexy scent washing over me as she zips her suitcase and yanks it off the bed. My chest constricts, and I wearily meet her eyes.

She searches my features, her expression softening. "Lucas, you really hurt me. You said you'd always be honest with me, yet you went behind my back. Trust is everything to me and you know that."

I gave her my heart, and she threw it away. "I admitted what I did! That was honest. Now sit next to me."

She eyes the bed and then me. "No."

"Why not?" I manage through my teeth.

"Because I'm mad at you, and you have no right to be mad at me and order me around."

"Please," I bite out. "I just want to talk."

"Fine." She sits a ridiculous distance away. "But only for a minute. I have to get to my signing."

I shift closer, determined to get to the bottom of this without losing my temper. "Alice, tell me why you, who are known for uplifting happy love stories, wrote this story where the scoundrel is never redeemed. He's miserable and alone at the end, stripped of everything that means anything to him."

She scowls, crossing her legs and smoothing her dress over them. "I don't want to talk about my story with you. The first draft isn't meant to be discussed or criticized. It's meant to be a raw messy outpouring."

My throat tightens. "Of you and your feelings."

She tilts her head. "Yes, in a way."

"But you said your readers want them to end up together, to be happy and in love. You need to fix it. Change the ending."

"You don't get a say in this! I don't care if you hate my story. It's mine." She exhales sharply. "The real issue is, how can I ever trust you again when you go behind my back?"

I scrub a hand over my face. "I'm sorry. I won't go on your laptop again. I wish I hadn't in the first place."

She shakes her head. "I just don't understand why you wanted to read it so badly."

Because I need answers. Because I'm yours, you have my heart, and I want you to be mine. I can't say it because it hurts too much to know I'm alone in this. "Because I was curious what you did with the fake engagement after ours," I finally say. "What about your readers? What about your editor? Do you care what they think? Because this story turns into a tragedy, and it hits that note hard."

She waves that away. "If my editor gives me any trouble, I'll add a five-years-later epilogue. After Diana has enjoyed her independence, she will fall madly in love with the gardener."

My gut does a slow roll. She'll leave, and then she'll move on. "Surely the gardener wouldn't be as interesting to her as the scoundrel?"

"She cares not for titles only for the good heart within." She's in her Regency speak as she thinks of her story. I know all her idiosyncrasies and love every last one of them.

"What if the scoundrel has a good heart within?" I press.

She shakes her head. "He doesn't. He's a scoundrel through and through. Unrepentant. Unreformable. He led her on and ruined her."

"Where is the happy ending?" I bark. "There has to be one! Write a better epilogue."

Her eyes flash. "Why do you care so much about the ending? You're not the writer here!"

"Because I love you!"

She holds up a palm. "Lucas, I just can't. I can't argue over the story you were never supposed to read, can't..." She takes a shaky breath. "I can't be with you anymore. I can't be with someone I don't trust."

My chest constricts, making it hard to breathe. I want to argue that she can trust me, but I know I was in the wrong. Just like I know she doesn't see committed love in her future with me.

She grabs her suitcase and walks out. A moment later, she pokes her head back in and shouts at the top of her lungs, "And there will be no epilogue with the gardener!"

I blink in surprise at the force of her words, as if I care so much about the gardener.

The moment she leaves, I flop back on the mattress and throw an arm over my stinging eyes.

Then I curl into the pillow that still smells like her and close my eyes, but I can still see the hurt in her eyes.

Alice

Lucas and I are through. And that is fine. Really. I'm fine. It. Is. Fine.

Without trust, there is nothing. And I wasn't ready for a heavy relationship, which he well knew, and so...this is all for the best. I paste on a smile, pretending to be following the conversation at the large round table, where I'm currently enjoying high tea with my readers. The British office of my publisher arranged this Sunday afternoon reader event at The Langham Hotel. I'm in the grand ballroom with two hundred readers and two debut historical romance authors I've only met for the first time today. After tea, the other authors, Sarah and Lauren, and I will take turns reading from our books, and then we'll do a signing. Tonight I'm supposed to have dinner with the British publishing team, spend the night, and leave the next morning. I have plane tickets back to the US from here tomorrow. That was the plan before Anna offered to let me stay the full six weeks to write my book. Now I don't know what to do. I want to return to the palace (you can't beat having servants to prepare meals while you write), but now with Lucas...I don't think I can.

I take a sip of tea to ease the tightness in my throat. Why did he have to do the one thing that would hurt me the most? Oh, I know it wasn't as bad as him cheating on me, which would be a low blow, but it was still a betrayal of my trust. The second time, too, and I can't let there be a third. I was just beginning to trust him enough to open my heart. Now it's clear he's the kind of man who does whatever serves his needs, even knowing it's the wrong thing. I suppose I should've known that since that's exactly what happened with our fake engagement. Gabriel told him no—his king!— and Lucas went through with it anyway.

What is wrong with men? Where is their sense of honor? This is why I prefer my old-school book boyfriends. They abide by a code of honor and always do the proper thing, except for the bedroom, where they're deliciously naughty. Lucas was a fantasy come true in that regard. *No thinking of naughty Lucas!* We are done. Capital D done. Stick a fork in it, we're done. And I'm fine with it. I'm a strong resilient woman who—

"Alice?"

I blink and look towards the brunette woman on my right. Olivia. She looks like she wants some kind of answer. "Yes, Olivia? Sorry if I spaced there."

She smiles prettily. "I was just saying I was sorry to hear about Mason. Are you okay? You haven't been on social media. Not that I'm a stalker!"

Mason. The name doesn't bring the sharp jab of pain it used to. I don't know if it's because I finally confronted him and said goodbye, or if it's because my mind has been so focused on writing my story and Lucas. *Ouch.* There's the jab of pain.

"Men suck," I announce, and the women around the table titter with surprise. "Except for book boyfriends."

A chorus of agreement goes around the table, and I smile. This is my second reader event in London, and I've found the readers to be wonderful.

"What's your next book about?" a blond woman across the table asks.

"William," I say. "It's called *The Scoundrel and the Governess.*"

"Ooh!" several women say.

"William is a scoundrel, how delicious!"

"I love the bad boys!"

"Does he seduce the governess, and they're forced to marry for propriety's sake?" Olivia asks.

Seven pairs of eyes stare back at me. *No, she's ruined by the end and so is he.* I can't say that. First of all, I never give away the ending. And second, why couldn't I write a happy ending? I saw myself in Diana, yet I couldn't give it to myself. I hoped for better, of course, which is why I thought of the epilogue. I just couldn't write the damn thing. Maybe, deep down, I no longer believe love always has a happy ending.

It's so much more complicated, messy, and imperfect. The real tragedy is that I didn't see the truth about love before. I press my fingers to my temples as a headache begins to throb.

A light hand touches my shoulder. It's Olivia. "Are you okay? Would you like some fresh air? There's a courtyard just through there." She gestures toward a door in the back of the room.

"No, I'm fine, thanks," I say. "Just a little tired."

Everyone gives me a sympathetic look, and somehow that makes me feel worse. I'm all off-kilter today, reeling from this morning's fight with Lucas. I have to power through. *Be the badass.*

"Back to your original question," I say to the women, "I never share the ending, but as soon as it's completed, in that lo-o-ong wait to publication, I'll start sharing teasers on my social media. And if you were one of the lovely readers who sent me a message of support after my ordeal with you-know-who, I thank you from the bottom of my heart. It really helped to make me feel less alone in my grief."

I pause, struck by that grief idea, dimly aware of more murmurs of support. I suppose it was like grief, losing Mason and Riley, and I feel better now because I had that goodbye, that sense of closure. I truly am a strong woman, not tough but resilient.

"I'm over the hump," I say. "Moving forward and back in my writing groove so I can get you more stories to read."

"Hear, hear!" Olivia cheers.

And then they toast me with their teacups, which is so darling. I relax and go back to enjoying finger sandwiches, pastries, and the wonderful company.

Once tea ends, the tables are cleared, and I go up to the head table with Sarah and Lauren. Sarah is American; Lauren is British. There's a podium with a microphone at the end of the table for our reading.

"I'm so nervous," Sarah whispers. "Why do I have to go first!"

"I'd trade places with you," Lauren says in a low voice, "but I don't want to go first either."

I'm supposed to go last because most of the readers are here for me, and the publisher wants them to give these new authors a chance with their full attention. "I was nervous my first time too," I whisper. "Just remember it's not about you. It's about your characters, and the readers want to hear what they're up to."

"That's a good way to think of it," Sarah says. "Did I mention my girl crush on you, or should I say author crush?"

I laugh. "Yes." Earlier, Sarah asked me to sign her Alice Segal books and gushed over me. I've done the same with favorite authors, so I totally get the excitement. "And now that I have your books, I can't wait to read them," I say to them both. "Just as soon as I'm past my deadline."

Sarah grabs my arm. "Oh my God, I have my first deadline. I'm so stressed. It took me five years to write my first book. How do you deal with the pressure?"

A voice at the podium catches my attention. It's the publicist from our publisher welcoming everyone.

"Email me," I whisper to Sarah. "Always happy to talk shop." Lauren gestures to herself, and I nod. "You too."

After the publicist introduces Sarah, I listen to her read a long excerpt from her story. Her voice is breathy, and she stops a few times to sip water, but she gets through it without passing out. I'm not saying I passed out at my first reading, just that I was a little light-headed.

Polite applause rings out, and she takes her seat, guzzling down the rest of her water. Lauren goes next, and her voice is fairly strong, so I return my attention to my book. I'm going to read an excerpt from *The Duke's Dare*. I love to read the first groveling scene out loud because it's funny, since the duke has never had to do anything so undignified before. Last time I was here I read from my more recent book *The Viscount's Victory* since it was a new release.

Lauren finishes and promptly sits down. I listen as the publicist introduces me, and try not to squirm. It's weird to hear someone talking about you when you're right there, especially if it's in gushing publicist speak.

I stand once she finishes, and the applause is deafening. I smile and head over to the microphone. "Wow. Thank you. All I had to do was stand and you ladies gave me a rousing round of applause. Guess I can go now." I fake heading back to my seat, stop, and shake my head. Everyone laughs.

I return to the microphone. "Seriously, thank you very much for the warm welcome. This has been such a wonderful experience with the high tea and meeting all of you and my new friends, Sarah and Lauren too. Weren't they wonderful? I can't wait to read their books. Definitely check them out after this and get them to sign your copy."

Sarah and Lauren beam at me, and I smile. I had plenty of support from more experienced authors when I was starting out and love paying it forward.

I hold up *The Duke's Dare*. "I'm going to read one of my favorite scenes for you. Can you guess which one?"

"Is it sexy?" someone hollers.

I laugh. "I think it's best if you read those scenes without hearing my voice in your head. Better to hear the duke's silky voice." I tuck my hair behind my ear, blushing even though I'm the one who wrote it. "I'll just get to it." I open the book and begin to read:

"Of course I should like to accompany you shopping." His voice *lowers to a silky purr. "After all, it was my fault your ribbon was misplaced."*

"Misplaced? You probably tied it to your bedpost as a souvenir!"

"He sounds like another scoundrel!" a masculine voice booms, startling me.

My head jerks up, and I gasp, my heart racing.

Several women whisper loudly, "Prince Lucas."

All eyes turn to him standing in the middle of the ballroom dressed in a light blue dress shirt and gray tailored pants. His hair is rumpled like he ran his fingers through it, the only sign of possible distress over our fight and breakup this morning. I can't believe he's here.

"Please continue," he says casually as if he isn't the only man standing in a room full of women romance readers.

His eyes belie his casualness, locked on mine in an intense fierce gaze. I gulp. Is he going to make a scene? He's already making a scene!

When I remain frozen in place, he goes on, still in his weirdly casual tone. "I know this story. The scoundrel fares very well, doesn't he?"

"Please sit down, sir," I say, adding politeness to the casual game and a dose of *I don't know this man.*

"Yes, ma'am," he says in feigned deference and sits on top of a nearby table. His guards shift closer to the table.

I smooth a shaky hand through my hair, desperately trying to get back on track. "Sorry. Where was I?" The words blur in front of my eyes, and I blink them back into focus. "I'll just begin again." I take a deep breath and begin to read, my voice not entirely steady.

"She should turn her back on him!" Lucas barks, standing again to face me. "And then she should leave him. That is what a scoundrel deserves."

I grind my teeth, sensing his metaphor between the two of us. I don't want to fight with him, even metaphorically, in such a public forum. "No. He did the wrong thing, took advantage, and now he is making amends."

He steps closer, and my heart thumps harder. "So *his* mistake can be fixed with a ribbon. But the other scoundrel… he gets nothing."

A low murmur goes through our audience. Dammit. My readers don't know a thing about the other scoundrel, and I don't want Lucas to give away any spoilers.

"Stop talking about scoundrels," I say firmly. "One of those stories isn't out yet." I smile at the audience. "No spoilers, right, ladies?"

"Are you and the prince together?" a woman shouts.

"No," I say at the same time as Lucas says, "Yes."

"Lucas!"

He strides forward, standing on the other side of the podium, his voice loud enough to carry. "I'm the scoundrel. You called me that before, so you must have known I would do the wrong thing, and I'm sorry." His voice cracks. "I will never, ever give you cause to doubt my honor again."

All eyes turn to me.

I blink and swallow over the lump in my throat. He's standing here in front of a crowd of women, groveling in his princely way, heart in his eyes, and I believe him. "Okay, Lucas. I accept your apology."

All eyes turn back to him, an excited whisper running through the room. Phones go up. This is going to hit social media. Crap.

"Thank you." He strides around the podium to my side. "Are you going to change the ending?" he demands in a tone so hostile I forget about everything but his awful misplaced fury. I'm the one who was wronged!

"Not because of you! It's my freaking story!"

He glares at me. "So you'll just leave me crushed beneath your heel, is that it?"

I suck in air. *Crushed beneath your heel.* He's mixing up our fight with the story. Diana says that in the story: *You crushed me beneath your heel and left. Why shouldn't I do the same?* And then it hits me. Lucas thinks he's William to me. I poured all of my anger and angst over Mason into this story. Mason is William, a version of him anyway. It is fiction.

I step away from the microphone so our conversation isn't broadcast to the world. "I wanted the beautiful garden scene in the epilogue. I just wasn't ready to write it. The gardener is kind and sensitive. He understands women's feelings. He listens and offers his friendship, which is how all the best relationships begin."

Lucas stares at me, his jaw slack.

My eyes sting, my throat tight. "And I hope that even if things were imperfect and complicated and messy, they would still be happy together."

He grabs me by the shoulders, his voice low and urgent. "Are you saying that I'm the gardener? The man she loves and lives with happily for the rest of her life?"

I nod, a tear escaping. "We did meet in the courtyard of the palace gardens."

He crushes me to him in a tight hug. Cheers go up around us. I hug him back, burying my face against his chest.

Someone says into the microphone, "Quiet, ladies, let's give them a moment."

The room goes silent. I belatedly feel self-conscious and try to pull away, but Lucas's grip is still tight. He missed me. I missed him too.

He whispers in my ear, "I'm so sorry I read your story without your permission. I just wanted an indication of your feelings, and I was being horribly impatient." He pulls back and frames my face with his hands. "Please forgive me, Alice. I've never felt this way before, never truly loved anyone before."

"Oh, Lucas, I forgive you. You don't have to keep grovel —err, apologizing."

"Princes don't grovel." He wraps his arms around my waist, drawing me close. "I want to marry you, and I know you're not ready. I'll wait. I swear I can be more patient as long as you're by my side."

A feminine voice says, "I'd at least consider marrying Prince Lucas."

I look around and realize many of the ladies in the audience have crept closer to get a better view of our no doubt interesting tableau.

Lucas nods emphatically. "It's what your readers want. You always say you want them to be happy with your stories."

I smile. "You are not my story, even if you are a gardener disguised as a scoundrel. You're so much more. You ring all my bells—princely gestures, a wonderful friend, and a beast in the bedroom."

He gives me his crooked smile, his eyes warm and tender.

A surge of affection has me throwing my arms around his neck and kissing him.

A cheer goes up from the women.

Lucas doesn't disappoint them or me, kissing me back passionately. When he finally lets me up for air, he touches his forehead to mine, his eyes intent. "I love you."

"I love you too," I manage over the lump in my throat. "So very much."

His eyes shine, and he presses his lips together like he's trying to hold back tears.

The room roars with approval—cheers, whistles, and applause so loud I almost want to take a bow. Except it wasn't a performance, it's my real life, and I know I want Lucas in it.

Lucas takes command, prince that he is. "Take your seats, ladies. It's time you hear this scene from a man with noble blood." He holds out his hand to me with a smile and guides me back to the podium. "You'll do the heroine's voice of course."

I can't help my smile. He respects and enjoys my work as a romance author—unlike most men—and he respects and enjoys me. I couldn't imagine a better man for me, and that's saying a lot considering my heroes are swoonworthy. Lucas is my-love-worthy, which is, for once, better than my imagination.

I join him at the podium, and we begin, our voices bantering, flirty and playful with an undercurrent of real sexual tension. He smolders down at me, and I flush hot in response.

We finish, and he takes my hand in a warm clasp as the audience cheers.

I finally found my hero, the prince of Villroy, the keeper of my heart.

EPILOGUE

Four weeks later...

Lucas

Alice is here to stay, and I couldn't be happier. Funny how just a small change of perspective—knowing she sees me more like the gardener at heart than the scoundrel reputation I've cultivated—has eased my impatience. Of course, her public declaration of love went a long way too. The internet exploded with our HEA (as Alice calls it), and her readers spread the word that I'm the scoundrel in her upcoming story. They love that it's based on a true love story. Her publisher immediately rushed out preorder listings for her book and promised an early release date. This set a fire under Alice, and she rewrote her draft in a frenzy of late nights, giving the scoundrel the heart of the gardener so he could ultimately have his happy ending. Like me. No, I didn't sneak read it. I only know this because she told me her plans right before she started her revisions. I'm respecting her privacy and her process. I haven't proposed either. I'm waiting (patiently) for her signal to know that she's ready.

I survey my palace suite, trying to see it from Alice's perspective. She turned in her book to her editor this morning, and this afternoon I moved her in. It's mostly antique mahogany furniture in the bedroom and a more contemporary feel in the living room with leather club chairs and glass tables. Not terribly feminine. I've never lived with a woman before, never wanted to. All she has with her is her laptop and a suitcase.

"You can add your personal touch," I tell her. "Whatever you want. Maybe with something from home." We'll head back to Oregon soon so I can meet her parents and she can pack her things and clear out her apartment.

She gives me her sweet smile, and my heart thumps harder. I don't know if I'll ever get used to those sweet smiles like sunbeams aimed straight at my heart. "I do have something from home with me. A gift for you."

"Really?"

She nods and digs into her suitcase, emerging with a small emerald ring. "It's too big for my finger since I lost weight, and I planned to have it resized, but I decided instead I'd really like you to have it." She hands it to me.

I close my fingers around the gift, unsure what it means or what to do with it. It's a woman's ring and too small for my own fingers. "Thank you."

She strokes my beard with an amused expression. "It's my birthstone ring. I bought it when I published my first book as a gift to myself, and now I would like you to have it as a promise ring, a symbol of my commitment that we'll be engaged in the future. I hope you like it better than the traditional hair ring." She grins. "Remember they did that in Regency times? The man wore a ring woven of his beloved's hair."

"I remember," I murmur, staring at the precious gift and then at her, barely able to speak over the lump of emotion lodged in my throat. "I will wear it on a gold chain every day as a constant reminder of your love."

She kisses me, wrapping her arms around my waist. "I'm yours, Lucas. And you're mine."

Sweeter words were never said.

"You're mine," I say hoarsely, wrapping my arms around her and nuzzling into her neck.

"Sweet Lucas."

I straighten and kiss her gently. "Sweet Alice."

Her blue eyes light up, her lips curving in a secret sexy smile. "Ravish me."

I give her a devilish grin and lunge for her. She laughs and races to the bed. I join her, covering her and kissing her smiling lips. Her hand cups my head for a passionate kiss, and raw desire spreads like fire in my veins. I slip her dress up and off, practically ripping the thing, all the while her hands are running over me, her mouth returning to mine again and again.

I pull back enough to strip my clothes off. "Get naked now."

She eagerly removes her bra and panties, flinging them to the side. We nearly collide in our eagerness to join skin on skin. She's ravishing me at the same time I'm ravishing her. We might kill each other in a wild frenzy of kisses and bites and strokes. I will die happy.

And then she's spreading her legs, pulling me closer, urging me on. "Now, Lucas, now."

I slide into heaven and groan, long and low. I gaze into her eyes, sharing a breath. "I love you."

Her fingers tighten at the nape of my neck. "I love you too, so, so much. You are my gift."

I close my stinging eyes, my throat tight. I'm the third-born son, which means I was not important to the crown. All I ever wanted was to be part of the kingdom's legacy and now I am. But this is so much more powerful. This is *every-thing*. I'm her gift. She loves me unconditionally just for being me.

I kiss her tenderly. "You are my gift, Alice. You are my life."

She kisses me passionately, her hips arching, taking me deeper. "I need you."

I pump slow and deep, my eyes never leaving hers. It

feels different now. I feel different, less frenzied and urgent. She's mine, and I want to cherish her, worship her, make love to her.

She smacks my ass. "Fuck me hard."

I grin, and then I do as the lady asks because I'm a scoundrel with a kind heart. She gasps and pants and chants my name, and then her nails dig into my shoulders, her body tightening around me, her head arching back, and I send her over the edge, her soft cries driving me on. I pump once, twice, and let go in an explosion of pleasure that rocks me, dimming the world to a haze of passion and love.

I collapse against her, pressing my lips to her neck. She holds me tight, and I'm content.

"Your love made me believe in happy endings again," she whispers.

My throat tightens. The woman is forever shooting arrows straight through my heart. I never stood a chance. Happily so.

I lift my head, and she gives me her sweet smile. "Your smile gave me joy, your belief in me gave me wings, and your love, darling, gave me the world."

She tears up. "And you said men don't spout poetry in the heat of passion. That was beautiful."

"I don't spout poetry," I say indignantly. "It's the happy afterglow talking."

She hugs me tight. "Then I look forward to more happy afterglows with you."

"Our future is filled with love, laughter, and *many* happy afterglows."

She pushes on my shoulders. "I need to get to my laptop. This is gold!"

I cradle her jaw. "Happy to be your inspiration; however, I have plans for you." I lower myself down her body, kissing along the way, and she sighs.

To entice Alice away from her laptop, I need to make her reality better than any fiction. I'll spend the rest of my life doing just that.

Don't miss the next book in the series *Royal Player*, where lightning strikes for Oscar!

Royal Player

Polly

I'm a modern twenty-three-year-old princess bound by rules more suited to medieval times. My father's declining health means I will soon be queen, but, as a woman, I will not be allowed to rule alone. I can only claim my birthright by marrying the man chosen for me—a business tycoon useful to our kingdom.

My parents are unbending. If I do not comply, my younger cousin will take my place simply because he's a man.

I'm the one who must bend, or walk away and lose everything—my family, my birthright, my island home.

I never met a man tempting enough to risk a kingdom… and then I meet *him*.

Oscar

I'm the good looking one. If you need to pick me out of the middle of the Rourke clan, that's how you do it. Does it bother me that nothing is expected of the fourth-born son other than to flash my devastatingly handsome smile for the press? Maybe.

Would I like to be needed even just by one person who sees me as key to something important? Yes.

And then I meet *her*.

Only lightning struck for the wrong woman. She's on Villroy for a short time before she must return home and marry the man her parents have chosen. If she doesn't, she loses her birthright.

If I truly care for Polly, I'll walk away. But do I have the strength to resist the most perfect woman I've ever met?

Sign up for my newsletter to be emailed when *Royal Player* releases at kyliegilmore.com/newsletter

ALSO BY KYLIE GILMORE

Happy Endings Book Club Series

Hidden Hollywood (Book 1)

Inviting Trouble (Book 2)

So Revealing (Book 3)

Formal Arrangement (Book 4)

Bad Boy Done Wrong (Book 5)

Mess With Me (Book 6)

Resisting Fate (Book 7)

Chance of Romance (Book 8)

Wicked Flirt (Book 9)

An Inconvenient Plan (Book 10)

A Happy Endings Wedding (Book 11)

The Clover Park Series

The Opposite of Wild (Book 1)

Daisy Does It All (Book 2)

Bad Taste in Men (Book 3)

Kissing Santa (Book 4)

Restless Harmony (Book 5)

Not My Romeo (Book 6)

Rev Me Up (Book 7)

An Ambitious Engagement (Book 8)

Clutch Player (Book 9)

A Tempting Friendship (Book 10)

Clover Park Bride: A Clover Park Short

A Valentine's Day Gift (Book 11)

Maggie Meets Her Match (Book 12)

The Clover Park STUDS Series

Almost Over It (Book 1)

Almost Married (Book 2)

Almost Fate (Book 3)

Almost in Love (Book 4)

Almost Romance (Book 5)

Almost Hitched (Book 6)

The Rourkes Series

Royal Catch (Book 1)

Royal Hottie (Book 2)

Royal Darling (Book 3)

Royal Charmer (Book 4)

Royal Player (Book 5)

Royal Shark (Book 6)

ABOUT THE AUTHOR

Kylie Gilmore is the *USA Today* bestselling author of the Rourkes series, the Happy Endings Book Club series, the Clover Park series, and the Clover Park STUDS series. She writes humorous romance that makes you laugh, cry, and reach for a cold glass of water.

Kylie lives in New York with her family, two cats, and a nutso dog. When she's not writing, wrangling kids, or dutifully taking notes at writing conferences, you can find her flexing her muscles all the way to the high cabinet for her secret chocolate stash.

Thanks for reading *Royal Charmer*. I hope you enjoyed it. Would you like to know about new releases? You can sign up for my new release email list at kyliegilmore.com/newsletter. I promise not to clog your inbox! Only new release info, sales, and some fun giveaways.

I love to hear from readers! You can find me at:
    kyliegilmore.com
    Instagram.com/kyliegilmore
    Facebook.com/KylieGilmoreToo
    Twitter @KylieGilmoreToo

If you liked Lucas and Alice's story, please leave a review on your favorite retailer's website or Goodreads. Thank you.

www.ingramcontent.com/pod-product-compliance
Lightning Source LLC
Chambersburg PA
CBHW070944180726
48291CB00004B/1130